A MEH-LIFE CRISIS

A MEH-LIFE CRISIS

jen parker

PROLOGUE

As Jane hid under the "Win a Free Pan" display table at her local
grocery store, she realized she had hit rock bottom. A heroin addict
stealing from his parents? Theresa May's Brexit deal? Those rock
bottoms had nothing on hers. Moments ago, clad in a dirty white
tank and oversized gray sweats, she had been picking up frozen
pizzas and copious bottles of wine as a fully adult 35-year-old is
wont to do. Passing by all of the Stepford families that populated
the Los Angeles grocery store, she scoffed all of the perfect 10s in
their couture yoga pants with their perfect angel twins, likely named
Ethan and Elijah or something similar.

And then she saw him. Her fucking ex-boyfriend Jason who
had broken up with her a mere six months before. The nerve of him

to be out in public when she looked so un-hot! So she did what any modern-day soldier of love would've done and hit the trenches.

At least she'd gotten away with it. He hadn't seen her dive for cover. She began to exhale a sigh of relief. But then he spoke. "Jane? I clearly saw you crawl under that table."

God damnit, she had been sighted by the enemy!

Thinking quickly, she retorted, "No I didn't." Hmm. Not an A+, but it was the best she had.

"Jane, can you come out of there?"

Reluctantly, she crawled out of her foxhole.

"Hi," she managed.

"Is that it? You dove under a table to avoid saying 'Hi'?"

Obviously. Who would want to be seen like this?

"Jane, are you ok?"

"Hell yeah. I'm killing it." She was categorically *not* killing it. Save for work, she had barely left her apartment in months.

"Ok. Well, I'll leave you alone. I just need to pick up a few groceries. It was good to see you."

As he walked away Jane slumped back under the table, contemplating her next move. She knew one thing. She had to make a move. Any move. She had nowhere to go but up.

* * *

A week later, Jane sat at a table in KC's Bar anxiously twirling her low-quality cabernet. As she awaited her crew-of-two, she was again pinged by thoughts of her grandmother's birthday party the night before. God, what the fuck was that all about? How the hell was she supposed to follow through on such a bizarre request. Did her grandma realize just how difficult this was going to be?

A familiar voice pulled her out of her head. Christine, dark hair falling messily out of a French twist, smoothed her blazer over her sides and slid into a chair. Jane was thankful her brother-in-law Paul had agreed to watch the kids so Christine could have a rare girls' night out. Jane knew Chris needed the break more than even she realized. Last night, she had just seemed distant. Very unlike the driven career woman she was, but Jane would get to the bottom of it. Before she had time to dive in, however, the bar door swung open and in walked her best friend. Effortlessly cool, Elle slid off her perfectly tattered leather jacket and grabbed a whiskey from the bar before joining her friends.

"Yo. Sorry I'm late. Traffic was a bitch today," Elle offered, sliding into the booth. She worked across town at the LGBTQ teen crisis center and kept late hours. She looked off too, even more than Jane would expect after sitting through a long commute. What was happening to Jane's group? Knowing better than to jump right in, she allowed banalities to ensue as the three caught up on life. With specifics not yet given, Jane would summarize the tone from all three as "everything sucks."

Not yet ready to dive deep into the undercurrent she was sensing, she turned to Christine. "By the way, what was up with Grandma last night?"

"The painting? She loved that thing."

"What painting?" Elle asked, trying to catch up.

Jane sipped her vino and said nothing.

"She asked Jane to find that painting from college she gave to Ridgeley." And there was Christine with the assist.

"What?" sputtered Elle. She and Jane hadn't met until years after college, but she was well aware of the tale.

"She wants me to find fucking Ridgeley," Jane said, staring at her friend blankly.

"She wants you to find the *painting*," Chris corrected.

"Same thing." Her grandmother's eightieth birthday was meant to be nothing more than a relaxing event with old people and cake. But after dessert Jane's father asked Grandma Jeannie if she had any wishes for her upcoming year. Grandma J once again joked that her biggest wish was for her heart to keep pumping and the family offered supportive laughter, as though they hadn't seen it coming from miles away. Then, her tone turned serious. Zoning in on Jane, she made a request that caused Jane to jump up from her seat: find the painting.

"But like, why?" Jane had shot back.

"That painting meant a lot to me. It actually meant a lot to your grandfather too. We talked about it quite a bit over the years. I'd like to have it."

Jane reminded her that she didn't have the painting anymore. It had, in fact, gone to her mortal enemy.

Clearing her throat, stalling to find words Jane would hear, Grandma exhaled. "Your Grandpa once told me that looking at that painting was the first time he got to see the whole you. I agreed. Christine is outgoing and friendly; she shows herself to the world daily. You, however, do not. Your Grandpa loved you two girls more than anything, and I do too. I want to see you, and I haven't for quite some time. I'd really like for you to find that painting and give it to me. Please." Sensing some hesitation in Jane, Grandma drove the final nail into the coffin. "Jane, I know it's a big ask, but I'm eighty. I don't have many wishes left. Please don't make me waste any."

And that was it. Jane was completely fucked. Granted, she

had been in a bit of a rut for past, say, few years. She could see the merit in embarking on a Reese Witherspoon-in-the-movie-Wild-like journey to find herself again. But finding Ridgeley? Ew.

"So now I've got to figure out how the hell to dig up a woman I've tried hard to forget for almost fifteen years.

I can't believe Grandma is doing this to me. Why didn't she just ask me to paint a new one? It'd be easier." Actually, that might've been worse. Jane hadn't painted in years.

"Well I can't believe I'm 37 and so single," Elle said, raising her glass to the group. "And dude. I only hang out with you guys. Shit, I need more friends." Jane knew that, despite her wry outburst, this was a sensitive subject for Elle. Open to both men and women, Elle had been hinting lately that she'd been thinking about settling down, but seemed unwilling to date. Jane suspected a mild case of baby-fever.

"Do you ever hear from Lilly?" Chris asked.

Elle tensed up. "I don't want to talk about me anymore," she said, downing the rest of her whiskey. She looked at Chris. "So Jane can't believe your grandma is an evil genius, I can't believe I'm so, so single…" She raised one perfect brow and Christine grabbed the proverbial mic.

"I can't believe I'm not sexy anymore. I need to start working out. Also, my marriage is stagnant and empty and I'm possibly not in love with my husband who might be cheating on me. I win."

"Whoa, wait what?" Jane asked. "When did this happen?"

"Paul and I are bored of each other. He's been working late lately. And early. All of the time. And his newest client is this hot new divorcée and I just feel it." Christine fiddled with her glass. "Something's going on. I think."

Jane and Elle exchanged a glance; Paul wasn't the type to cheat. But regardless, Chris was clearly unhappy.

Jane's eyes flashed and she stood up with zest. "Fuck it, you guys. Let's not take this shit lying down! Let's do something about it."

"Like what?" Elle asked.

"Well," Jane started, "Elle, you could start dating." Elle stared back blankly. "I know you've got plenty of experience with hook-up apps but if you want a serious relationship, you have to take matters into your own hands. You have to date differently. And by 'date' I mean actual relationships, not one-night stands."

"Shit," Elle grumbled.

"Because this is L.A. most people are gonna be lame," Jane added empathetically. "They'll, like, eat kale and talk about self-care. Oh, and they'll for sure reference 'The Universe.' I know that drives you crazy. But you need to try anyway. There's got to be at least a few normal people in this city. Download an app or something. And *not* a hook-up app, an actual dating app. And don't sleep with them until at least three dates in. Talk to them first." Elle rolled her eyes, but the gesture did nothing to hide her consideration of the idea. "And date women. I think you connect better with them than men." Jane knew Elle might not be ready for that one, but she had to throw that out there. "I don't know why you feel you need more friends because face it, we're the shit, but if the date doesn't work out on a romantic level at least you'll be going out and meeting people. Win-fucking-win."

Jane turned her attention to her sister. "And you. If you're bored in your marriage, do something about it. Spice it up. Make yourself feel sexy. You don't need to work out, but if you think it'll make you feel better then go join a gym. With the money you two make, that shouldn't be hard." She ignored Christine shifting uncomfortably. "Do whatever you have to do to re-invest in the relationship. Take a romantic cruise for two. Go on nightly walks on the beach. Sign up for ballroom dance lessons or some cheesy shit. I don't know. I'm probably talking out of my ass," Jane took another sip of alcoholic goodness. "Also, he's not cheating on you!" she practically yelled. "Anyone with eyes can see that."

Her motivational speech was enthusiastic, though Jane realized she might be going a little overboard. What was in these drinks?

"And me. I'm sick of sitting on my ass, wishing things would come to me. They're not going to come to me. Fuck it. I'll go get the painting and take my fucking life back from the bitch who stole it in the first place!" Jane was full blown shouting with excitement. "WHOOO!" She looked at Elle and Chris. Why weren't they cheering?

"I mean, she didn't really..." Christine started.

"Yeah, no one can take your life..." Elle continued.

Jane stopped them. "Oh, shut the fuck up and cheers!"

With that they clinked glasses, committing to taking their lives back in whatever way they could.

Once they figured out how.

CHAPTER ONE

After a long day of passionless work, Jane sat on her couch pondering her first move toward finding the painting. She had succumbed to the fact that she'd have to find her college nemesis; now she needed to figure out how to do it. The hard part was she didn't know the woman's last name. Ridgeley was one of those people that went by one name only, as though she were Cher.

She was so *not* Cher.

Jane was also relatively sure Ridgeley was a made-up first name, because really, who named their kid *Ridgeley*? Thus, Jane really didn't know the woman's first or last name. Great.

She grabbed a notebook, ready to outline a plan, and wrote "Finding Ridgeley" across the top of the first page. Step one was obvious. "Google," she murmured as she wrote. She'd Google the crap out of her. After all, even if Ridgeley was a fake name, she might still be using it for her art.

If a simple internet search didn't pan out, she'd move on to step two. "Facebook." Granted, any Facebook pictures would likely come up in a Google search but it was still worth a shot. Also, even if she couldn't find Ridgeley directly, with Facebook she'd find mutual friends who were sure to know where she was.

Step three. Hmm. If all else failed, go to UCLA and beg the registrar to look her up? Jane crossed that off the list. It probably wouldn't pan out. What would she even say? "Can you look up someone named Ridgeley whose name probably isn't Ridgeley?"

It didn't matter. In this day and age, it was extremely unlikely that finding her would take more than steps one and two.

Proud of herself for making the list, Jane poured herself a glass of celebratory wine and continued on.

She grabbed her laptop and opened her browser. With bated breath, she typed in the word Ridgeley.

The search results were not what she was hoping for. Almost all of them were for Andrew Ridgeley, the other guy from *Wham!* Other than that, she saw a few random apartment complexes with Ridgeley in the name and that was it. Not deterred, she added the word "art" to the search. More Andrew Ridgeley hits. She tried "artist." Andrew from *Wham!* again.

Well then.

This might be a while.

She went down as deep of a dive as she could, adding various search words to the name but nothing popped up.

With an audible sigh Jane switched gears: Facebook time. Damn, Andrew Ridgeley again. She began to search through friends' friend lists. Of course, it didn't help that Jane really hadn't stayed in touch with many people from college. A few acquaintances had tried to friend her at one point but she rejected them because she didn't know them well. No need to clog her newsfeed with pictures of food and memes about living, loving, and laughing! Unfortunately, now she couldn't even remember their names, which made it pretty hard to search for them.

But there *was* one name she remembered well. She had never looked for him before, not even an innocent little internet stalking. Bile rose in her stomach, and she inhaled deeply in attempts to settle it, or at least force it back down. Into the search bar she typed D-A-V-E S-P-E-N-C-E-R. Should she hit enter? Could she stand to see what he'd been up to all these years? Did she really want to know?

Fuck it. She hit enter.

Four or five Dave Spencers filled her screen and as she glanced down the column, there he was. With the same curly hair, a few of them graying, with a few more distinguishing wrinkles staring right back at her, but it was the same Dave. Dave the Heat, she had called him. *Do you know Dave?* Mark Zuckerberg asked her tauntingly through text right under the photo. She wished there were an "it's complicated" button for that one.

Dave looked so happy. In his profile picture he had a knit beanie on his slightly overgrown curly hair, a skater t-shirt, and an adorable little blonde girl on his shoulders.

"Holy shit, Dave has a daughter!" She was filled with competing emotions: amusement that he'd settled down; anger thinking back to college and how he'd hurt her; sorrow that she'd missed something so important. With the realization that her best friend from a lifetime ago still existed, Jane felt a piece of herself return. She pushed aside the lingering sadness as she admitted she could have collected it at any point she'd wanted.

Jane clicked on the *About* section. Studied at UCLA, which she already knew. And everything else was marked *Ask Me*. Ugh, Dave.

She clicked on the *Friends* section. Damnit Dave! He had a famous person's level of friends, meaning every time a bot or an unknown bored person in Cambodia friend requested him, he'd said yes. This boded well for the odds of his accepting her friend request, but it made the task of scrolling through his friends to find the elusive Ridgeley much more difficult. Smiling wryly to herself that it couldn't be that easy, Jane typed in Ridgeley's name.

It wasn't that easy.

Jane sighed. Keeping loose ties with other people from college would have been pretty clutch right now. Oh, well. She would pillage Dave's friend list until she got tired, then she'd woman up and message him.

Scrolling through, she did recognize a couple of people she had forgotten. Matt McKinley? Oh yeah, Dave had been friends with him freshman year. What ever happened to him? Jane clicked on his picture. Married with kids. She went back to Dave's page. Shea D'Angelo? She'd lived in Dave's dorm freshman year. What happened to her? *Click.* Married with kids. Ugh. Back to Dave. Fill Damien. Oh my God, Phil *still* spelled his name "Fill"? He had been Dave's roommate freshman year. *Click.* Married with kids.

This was starting to become a pattern.

Having had enough, Jane scrolled through the rest of Dave's

friends list, which was a commitment in and of itself. When Jane finally reached the end, she let out a sigh of relief. None of them was Ridgeley. Fuck. But thank God. But fuck. Not knowing what to do next, she poured herself a hefty glass of red wine and brought her laptop to the couch. "Fuck it," she said as she hit *Request Friend.* With that, she shut her laptop and began watching bullshit TV.

At least she'd taken the first step. Hell yeah.

* * *

Elle sat in her apartment feeling lost and not knowing where to begin. She had always considered herself to be quite sexually liberated. She never cared about the standard slut-shaming that went on in college, or the so called "walk of shame" back to her dorm after a night of fun decisions. Her mother had raised her to think for herself and not worry about the judgements of others, so Elle had banged her way through college as much or as little as she felt like, and graduated with plenty of sexual experience under her belt.

Elle also had never had a strong preference for males or females. She enjoyed both for different reasons. Men were a way to have her needs met, but they weren't people to settle down with. In her experience, men lacked emotional intelligence. Whenever she'd want to talk something through men would just want to fix it. Also, they had a very predictable 'can we have a threesome' type response when they found out she was bisexual. Ugh.

Women, on the other hand, not only knew how to work a girl sexually, but they also understood the need for intimacy and emotional connection. A good woman was a best friend, lover and therapist all rolled into one. Yes, Elle usually had better luck with women. At least, until Lilly.

But it still hurt to think about her, so Elle shoved the memories aside.

In order to stop the one-night stands she needed to look for something different. But what? And how? Besides not using hook-up apps, she had no idea how to go about pursuing a relationship.

Lilly had always talked about a book called *The Knowledge*. It was a best-selling self-help book. She'd bought Elle a copy and, after enough pressure from her, Elle had read it, hoping to find something to like about it.

It was utter bullshit.

First of all, it talked about The Universe non-stop: "Be careful of negative thoughts you put out into The Universe. You never know what it will manifest." That kind of hippie, new-age crap. Second, it clearly meant to spread the obvious message that if you focus on what you want, you're more likely to get it. It also offered the misguided yet trite implication that deep-down people knew what they wanted, and that getting what they want would make them happy. Bullshit.

Putting the negativity aside, Elle remembered the book did have one good idea and that was to write out a list of goals and meditate on them. Though she'd skip the meditation part, Elle reasoned that if she created a list of what she wanted in a partner, she could rule people out who didn't meet her needs. Something practical like this might serve her better than following her gut feelings. After all, clearly her gut sucked when it came to dating. She took out a pen and wrote: *Is fun. Wants a relationship.*

There. That wasn't so bad. It's not like Elle was asking for a lot in a partner, after all. Reading over her list, she realized something major was missing. *Wants kids.* Yeah, that was an important one. She was thirty-seven. And her clock was ticking.

Taking a sip of wine, she glanced at her copy of *The Knowledge* and added a final bullet point: *Doesn't talk about The Universe.*

With that, she put the list on the table and downloaded her first dating app.

* * *

At Christine's house, things were actually quiet. Cameron and Lucy were finally in bed and Paul was, of course, still at work. She turned on the television and tortured herself with self-comparisons to the actresses on screen. Why did she feel so frumpy lately? Granted, she wasn't her 20-year-old self anymore, but would she feel this way if Paul were spending more time at home? He had a stressful job as a divorce attorney, but his recent time away sure coincided nicely with taking on Angela as a client.

With the TV on as background noise, she also began to scroll through social media. A post by a much younger and extremely attractive co-worker of hers made her smile. Frankie, a young realtor new to her office, had booked a new listing. Good for him! Looking at the picture of him giving a goofy thumbs up, she immediately felt humiliated. Here was a good-looking pup, new to the job and with a zest for life. By comparison she was a wrinkled old dog with excess weight along with other baggage.

What had become of her? Was this how she planned to live her life, giving up on herself and her happiness? Chris shook her head. Her husband's whereabouts may be out of her control but there was one thing she could do to make herself feel better. A few clicks on her phone, and small damage to her credit card later, she downloaded an app and joined her first gym.

Christine tossed and turned in bed that night until Paul crawled in at around eleven.

"Where have you been?" a sleepy Chris asked her potentially cheating husband.

"Work. I told you, things are really crazy right now."

Paul did work hard to provide for his family. Which Chris appreciated, truly. But as Paul settled into bed Chris caught a faint whiff of perfume. "Were you with Angela?" she couldn't help but ask.

Paul sighed, "Yes. Working. She insists on going over every little detail of their assets."

Was that the truth? Or did that sneaky little tart just come up with reasons to get Paul alone? And was he receptive to it? Christine just wasn't sure, but she didn't feel like getting into it this late. So instead of the confrontation she wanted, she rolled over, stuffed down her tears, and tried to get the sleep she needed.

CHAPTER TWO

The next morning, Jane peeled herself out of bed. She considered checking Facebook to see if Dave had accepted her friend request but she was too nervous. She'd allow 48 hours from the time she sent it before she checked again. That way she could go to work, spend a reasonable amount of time freaking out, and then settle in on the couch for either excitement or disappointment.

Jane ploughed her way through her work day at Hudson Solutions, the market research firm where she'd been employed for the last ten years. She serially avoided contact with most co-workers except Todd, the snobby receptionist. He'd make snide remarks about her clothes being inappropriate for a professional environment, and she'd tell him he was the full body version of resting bitch face.

It was their thing.

Toward the end of her day, bored with the content of emails and Buzzfeed, she allowed her mind to wander back in time to the days of college, art, and Dave the Heat, whose very presence knocked the wind out of her and kept her begging for more.

Dave was a college girl's wet dream. He was a poet who played guitar, and his emotions ran so deep he would at times cry at the sight of a beautiful sunset. 35-year-old Jane would laugh him right out of an open-mic night, but 18-year-old Jane fell head over heels in love with him. He "got her" in a way others didn't. He was an English major with a passion for creative writing. He loved chai tea and Kerouac, because of course he did. Dave was the kind of guy one assumed smoked weed, but he didn't because he "didn't want his well of emotions covered by anything impure." Oh, Dave.

The day they met was like something out of one of his poorly-written stories. Jane noticed him first, all that curly hair hidden under a backwards grandpa hat. His starry eyes full of heat, staring at her intently. His swaggering walk, proclaiming his confidence. And the first word this God uttered to her? "Hey."

"H-hey," Jane stuttered back.

"You're the art chick. I dig your style."

At that, 18-year-old Jane climaxed. (Mentally; come on, it was never that easy.)

And so their friendship began. They'd go to art shows and coffee houses and discuss the deeper things in life, things like if she saw something blue, was it the same blue to him? Jane turned him on to hippie-rock and he introduced her to underground punk.

There were deeper feelings there under the surface but it was complicated. Ok, it wasn't complicated: Dave had a girlfriend. A pre-law girlfriend in Chicago.

Still, their friendship—platonic on his side, infatuated on hers—continued.

Dave would take her on "discovery walks" every day. They'd wind around campus, looking for over-looked surprises like a piece of gum on a sidewalk in the perfect shape of a diamond, a park bench broken symmetrically down the middle, or a trail of dog footprints that seemed to simply vanish into the beauty of the winter. Jane would invite Dave to the art building where he'd watch her paint, listening to *Diamonds and Rust* by Joan Baez and various Fleetwood Mac songs on repeat. Jane could get lost in her painting for hours. She used it as a vehicle to show her true self to the world, and more importantly, to discover herself. Dave watching her paint was a huge boost to her confidence. But even as he raised her sense of worth something else gnawed at it: a fellow art student named Ridgeley. The ethereal, wistful blonde quickly became Jane's arch nemesis. When it boiled down to it, Jane couldn't come up with a good reason to hate her except for one, and it was a big one.

Ridgeley was a better artist than Jane. By a lot.

Ridgeley's paintings were *full* of personal voice and an effort-lessness that made Jane green with envy. Less technical than Jane's, they were infused with feelings Jane hadn't experienced, or maybe ones she hadn't dared to access. Ridgeley could condense a moment in time into a few brush strokes so accurately the viewer felt a part of the painting. For this, everyone praised Ridgeley's talent.

And Jane wanted to claw her face off.

She'd often offset her simmering rage with doses of Dave. He was addictive. She had to be near him. But he had a girlfriend that they rarely talked about.

So they continued as they were, Dave blissfully unaware of Jane's romantic feelings.

Jane started drinking chai tea on a daily basis. Dave started wearing glints of silver, like a chain or an earring. They were becoming one, enmeshing themselves so deeply in each other's lives that an invitation extended to one was an implied invite to the other. Jane started to study creative writing while Dave enrolled in a drawing class, one that unfortunately had Ridgeley as the Teacher's Assistant. Ew.

Jane was imploding under the weight of sheer love for Dave. She'd often go running to help dissipate the energy. She found herself short of breath when he'd walk in the room. She'd wake with a jump in the night from the sexual heat of her dreams. But Dave had a girlfriend.

A full six months into their friendship, Jane dipped back in, testing the girlfriend waters.

"So, when is Mandy coming to visit?"

"Oh. Mandy and I broke up," Dave mentioned casually.

Jane froze. Oh my God, this was her chance. She sat on the edge of her chair, the weight of the moment propping her up so she didn't tip over. She was pulled by competing urges. Should she pounce on him or console him?

"When did that happen?" Nice and casual. Not bad, Jane.

"Just last week. I told her I was developing feelings for someone else. She didn't love that."

Holy shit. "Oh? Um. Ok. Who?"

Here it was. It was coming. This was the moment she had been waiting for.

"You're not going to like this."

Oh, she'd definitely like this. "Is it m—" Jane began to ask.

"It's Ridgeley."

NOOOOO! The name uttered from Dave's mouth hit Jane like a ton of bricks.

"Jane, you don't even know her. I really think you'd like her."

Dave knew. He *knew* Jane was anti-Ridgeley. Granted, he may not have known exactly how much, as Jane generally didn't taint her conversations with The Heat by infusing their talks with wretched Ridgeley. But he knew. And she had really thought this was going to be Dave's moment to make a move on *her*.

"What the fuck, Dave?!"

"Whoa. Dude."

"Fucking Ridgeley! How did this not come up until now?"

"I don't know. You and I don't talk about stuff like this. Plus, I know you're jealous of her."

Oh, holy hell. It was on now. "Jealous of her? Why would I be jealous? Because she has everything that I want?" Ok, perhaps jealous was an accurate term. Dave had to subconsciously know Jane was in to him, had to have known that she felt an umbilical connection to his very soul. He was not getting away with this. "Seriously fuckhead, do you not know why we 'don't talk about stuff like this'? Do you not know that I'm into you? Like so, so into you!"

Dave's face went blank. "You are? Why didn't you ever say anything?"

"Because you had a fucking girlfriend." Tears began to fight their way through the last layer of Jane's wall.

"Oh."

Yeah. Oh. He really hadn't known.

But the damage was done. Jane was shaken by the bitterness of Dave's betrayal. The puncture wound had already started to bleed out, and the blood tasted of Ridgeley. And of course Ridgeley was into Dave too. Who wouldn't be? As Dave and Ridgeley began to knit together, Jane unraveled. The injustice killed her. Ridgeley had taken every art accolade Jane could have hoped to receive. She took the praise of professors and peers. All of that Jane hated, but she could deal with it. But this? Ridgeley had taken from Jane the very thing she could not lose. And Dave had willingly walked toward her.

Jane began cooling herself off from The Heat. It was the only way she could tolerate moving forward. She traded in her chai for black coffee. She dropped out of creative writing, telling the teacher that she had to go to rehab (you know, college logic). In a way, she *was* in rehab; she was suffering serious withdrawals from her favorite drug.

She turned to painting as her only solace. Finally, her art reflected real emotion. She didn't want to see her own pain on the page, but she couldn't help it. Her body could no longer fit the depth of her longing for Dave, nor could it withstand the razor-sharp stab of his lack of passion for her. Thankfully, her art was there to soothe her. Painting carried her through the aching hours in the middle of the night, which her poor young heart didn't understand only time could relieve.

To add to the pain, "Ridgeley" was a name Jane continued to hear in her classes. A glimmer of hope finally came at the end of sophomore year when Jane found out her final exam in Painting 302 would include a competition across classes. Jane knew her work had taken on new depth. She knew it told stories that her previous self couldn't bear to have shown. This was it. She could finally beat Ridgeley.

Jane spent days and nights thinking about what she'd paint, starting pieces and scrapping them, going back to the canvas again and again. How could she best vomit her feelings onto the page, and how much bile was she willing to show the world?

In the end, she decided to go for broke. The best way to move past something was to stare it in the face, embrace it, then let it go. She poured her soul into the painting, the smell of the acrylics cushioning her mind. She started with hues of blue and silver, and slashed in harsh tones of red and black. She used actual dirt to muddy the look and show the weight of what she carried. When she finally finished, she looked at her piece. Pain on the page.

Her eyes welled up. It was fucking perfect.

When competition day arrived, Jane did a quick walkthrough of the show space. She caught glimpses of the other works, but she didn't take much time to review.

Until she got to Ridgeley's. It was a whir of crystallized pastels, with white glitter as the overarching color. Ethereal and beautiful, as always. But for the first time in a long time Jane was hopeful. Her own work was better. It was guttural and raw. The true point of art was to incite feeling after all, and Jane's work did that more than Ridgeley's.

She was going to win.

Jane allowed herself to enjoy the event. Her family and friends were there, after all. She clung to her grandparents until the judging commenced. With the confidence of an NBA first draft-pick, she stood proudly, waiting for the news.

The judges said some general pleasantries about the level of talent shown in the competition before they finally got down to it. Here was her moment. Chills ran up her back as she braced herself for glory. "Second runner up, goes to…Tyler Franson." She took a breath knowing she was one step closer. "This was a close competition folks. There's lots of talent on display here. But without further ado, your first runner up is…Jane Baker, and the winner of the competition is Ridgeley."

No! It couldn't be!

Each "good job, Jane" she heard put another pin prick in her. She struggled to keep it together. Then all of the sudden, she heard a voice that made her want to scream. "Hi Jane."

Fucking Ridgeley.

Jane turned and stared pure venom at the girl in front of her. "Jane, I know you're not a big fan of mine." Good. At least she got that. "I just wanted to say, honestly, your piece is amazing. You really should have won."

Fuck this. "Don't patronize me, Ridgeley."

Ridgeley looked surprised. "No, I'm not. I mean it. Your painting is better than mine. I honestly think the judges assumed I'd win and it muddied their judgment. Yours is better. It actually brought tears to my eyes."

Jane felt pure poison in her veins. "Yeah, well, you can have it."

Ridgeley looked taken aback. "Really? Jane, I would love that."

"It's yours." With that, Jane walked away. She wanted to crawl out of her skin but she'd settle for crawling into her bed and burying herself under the darkness of her blankets.

"Thanks," she heard Ridgeley call after her. What the fuck? Even Ridgeley knew she should have won and yet, it didn't matter. With that bitch around, she just could not win.

And if she couldn't even beat out a rival at the collegiate level, she didn't stand a fucking chance in the world of professional art.

Before the start of the next semester, Jane changed majors, despite her advisor's horror she'd switched at the start of junior year. Sure, Jane felt like a coward for doing it but cowardice was more tolerable than pain. And something safe like Marketing would ensure she wasn't continually exposed to the pain of realizing she was a failure.

Life moved on. But maybe Jane hadn't.

Brrrring. The ringing phone brought her back to the present. It was Todd so she sent it to voicemail.

Snapping herself back into work mode, she shook off her past and managed to stay on task until the end of the day.

CHAPTER THREE

Knowing she had to steer clear of hook-up apps, Elle downloaded Buzz. Buzz was a swiping app, but its schtick was that if a (hetero) match was made, the woman had to start the interaction. Fine by Elle; she definitely wasn't shy.

Without much thought she set up a profile. Pulling photos was easy since the app could link to social media. In the "About Me" section she paused. Being a woman of not too many words, she went with: *Social Worker, Chill, No hook-ups.*

She began swiping away. A few seconds in, she got a buzz. The guy was decent looking in a beachy-yet-rugged sort of way, which she dug.

She sent a screenshot to Jane.

I see you're into Owen Wilson, she texted back.

Elle cracked a smile. He *was* an Owen Wilson type. His bio said he'd just moved back to L.A. from the Mid-West with a back-pack. He was couch surfing until he sold his house in Wisconsin and made the move official.

Clocking all of this as potentially sketchy, Elle reasoned that if he owned a home, he must have some of his shit together. She took out her list: *Is fun. Wants a relationship. Wants kids. Doesn't talk about The Universe.*

He certainly looked fun. It was too soon to ask about rela-tionships and kids and she'd only know the last one if she started a conversation, so Elle took a chance and sent him a message.

Hey. A backpack, huh? Not even a suitcase? Damn, you must've wanted to leave the Mid-West.

He responded right away.

Sup Elle? Yeah, shit there got lame so here I am. Fancy meeting up sometime this week?

Well, that was quick. Elle was about two minutes into her app dating phase and she'd already hooked a fish. She hit the pause button on him and kept swiping and messaging. When she checked the app later that night, she'd received messages from three men, each ignoring the questions she had posed in her original message and instead responding with "How is your day going?"

Quickly realizing Owen was the most interesting fish she'd caught thus far, she responded to his request. *Sure. I live West. You? Maybe we can meet in the middle.* Elle knew men were supposed to be willing to travel for the first date, but she wanted to be cool. Meeting in the middle was a reasonable compromise.

I'm downtown. Mind if we meet up by me? I don't have a car.

Hmm. Strike one. His bio referencing couch surfing meant he was technically without a permanent place to stay. In the world of social work, this was called "experiencing homelessness." Jane would have definitely just called it "homeless." So maybe he was Owen Wilson in a *You, Me and Dupree* kind of way. Crashing downtown and not having a car screamed at least homeless-adjacent, but the guy did own property in Mid-America. So he wasn't fully homeless. He was Almost (Experiencing) Homeless(ness) Owen Wilson.

It was beyond annoying that he wasn't willing to take the train to meet her half way, but nonetheless Elle was too curious to be out. He might be some hipster investor waiting to figure out his next move. Or he might be kind of homeless. If nothing else, meeting up with this guy would be a rep under her belt. Plus, she had a good feeling some great stories could come out of this.

No problem, she replied.

Owen Wilson suggested meeting up at a hipster ice cream place in the arts district and Elle agreed. She arrived a few minutes early and scoped out the place. He definitely wasn't there yet. A few minutes in, she spotted a rugged blonde guy approaching with a wry smile and she knew it was him.

Hmm. Judging by his outfit, she could not fully rule out the homeless theory.

"'Sup girl. You're a babe, good on you," he said as he gave her a side-hug. So this guy was a surfer-hippie. She enjoyed how non-threatening his presence was. They talked about the weird-ass ice cream flavors like honey suckle-lavender and mint julep until they reached the front of the line. The gender non-conforming cashier took their orders. Elle went with toasted caramel and rose because it sounded so bad it had to be good, and Almost (Experiencing) Homeless(ness) Owen Wilson went with Earl Gray infusion. At the register Elle paused, not sure how to handle the transaction. She figured Owen was supposed to pay because he had asked for the date, but she didn't want to be presumptuous. As the cashier looked-up, Owen piped up. "We'll pay separate."

Well, ok then. Elle fronted her own four dollars for the ice cream and grabbed a glass of water.

Owen pitched the idea of taking a walk, which Elle jumped on. In fact, walking through different areas of the city and exploring different holes-in-the-wall was how she spent a lot of her free time. As they wandered down some streets she'd been down a thousand times, she probed a bit about his situation.

"So, what is it you do exactly?" That felt like an inoffensive way to get at her bigger questions.

Owen explained that back in Wisconsin he had been a free-lance copywriter. That was a real job, so he had that going for him. He'd lived in L.A. about five years ago and moved to the Mid-West for work. The main company who'd contracted him had recently closed, and he couldn't stand the thought of another Wisconsin winter so he decided to up and move back on a whim.

Elle considered herself a bit of a free spirit. But not to this degree.

Owen mentioned he was crashing with a bunch of ex-girl-friends and he was lucky they were successful and had space for him in their places. Huh. Surprising he was willing to admit it. It made him sound like a complete taker.

When she asked him what he hoped to do for work in L.A., he mentioned he wanted to buy some land in the suburbs and build a house.

For himself.

His career plan was to build a house. For himself. And not sell it.

Elle clocked the fact that he seemed to not understand what "work" meant.

Owen asked Elle some questions about herself. By this point she knew she had no romantic interest in him, but, in the interest of being fair, she decided to continue the date.

Plus, she had tons of curiosity.

She asked him how he spent his days, thinking the logical answer would be house hunting or working toward putting his Mid-West place on the market. Instead, he mentioned that he spent the bulk of his daylight hours walking around and looking at things, the artsy way to say "I do nothing." And there was strike two.

Once she had her fill of his surfer boy, artsy, not-doing-anything-with-his-life conversation, Elle decided to end the date, but Owen beat her to the punch. Oh, thank God. At least he realized they had nothing in common and she wouldn't have to deal with having the "thanks but no thanks" conversation.

As they approached her car, Elle could feel his next words coming. *He's going to ask me for a ride. There's a 100% chance this dude is about to ask me for a ride.*

"Hey, any chance you can drop me off at Union Station?" he asked, as if on cue.

Having categorized him early as a non-threat, Elle acquiesced. She wasn't afraid of this guy, but she did think it was lame he couldn't walk his own ass to the train station. Oh well. This would be the last she'd see of Almost (Experiencing) Homeless(ness) Owen Wilson.

But on the way to the station, Owen indicated he had a different point of view. "I had a great time tonight! We should do this again! I'll hit you up!"

Unsure if he was just saying this out of politeness or not, Elle smiled and offered a non-committal "cool."

"Feels like the Universe brought us together, you know?"

There it was. Strike three. When she got home, she poured herself a whiskey in celebration of getting the fuck out there and doing the damn thing. Sure, her first date had been with a by-choice semi-homeless person, but hey, she had gone on a date. More than that, she had gone home alone.

Elle pulled out her list and added to it: *Not experiencing homelessness. Financially responsible.*

* * *

Later that night Elle went to Jane's to watch some bad TV and fill her in on the saga. She allowed Jane to laugh and wince in pain at her adventures. But after a bit, Elle realized she was the only one laughing at the Real Housewives of Nonsense County.

"Dude, what's up with you?" Elle asked.

Jane had been avoiding Facebook since she friend-requested Dave a couple days ago. Now, with Elle at her side, she was actually ready to check it. Jane filled Elle in on the friend request situation.

"Damn. Ok. Let's do this."

With that, Jane mustered up some false courage and opened the Facebook app on her phone.

Oh my God he'd accepted her friend request! Her stomach and heart jumped in unison as she yelled and Elle smiled. This was big. The shocking realization that he still existed hit her again like wave, knocking her off kilter. Dave Spencer was real and not just in her memories.

She looked to the top right of her screen and clicked the now blue icon. "Holy shit, he sent a message!" she whisper-screamed as she clicked on the text and read aloud: "Wow. What a blast from the past. You know, I've thought about reaching out to you over the years but wasn't sure how you'd take it. It's so good to see your face. You look as pissy as ever:) Hope you're well. Hope to hear back from you. Love always, Dave"

"Holy fuuuuck!" she exclaimed as Elle refilled her wineglass. She couldn't even drink it she was so amped up. Once Jane caught her breath, Elle asked if she wanted her to stay or go. Jane knew she was ready to respond and she kind of wanted to do it alone. Elle hugged her and gave her some words of encouragement, specifically "You got this bitch," and took off.

Jane smiled as a tear dripped down her cheek. Was she ready for this? To re-kindle a friendship with Dave? And he had said "love always." Did that mean they were cool? "Slow down," she told herself out loud. It had been almost fifteen years and this was just a Facebook message. It didn't mean she and Dave would be friends. It meant they'd be Facebook friends and there was obviously a big difference. She poised herself to respond.

Dave. Holy fuck, you still exist. I have tons of questions but first, I'm on a bit of a mission and need some help. Are you still in touch with Ridgeley?

Dave responded immediately. She hadn't even noticed the green dot by his name, indicating he was on Facebook right now.

Janey, oh Janey. You haven't changed a bit. Ridgeley. Wow that's a name I haven't thought of in years.

Jane's heart skipped. And really, what the fuck was *that* about?

Oh really? What's her last name? I know this is weird- I'm trying to find a painting she has of mine. Also, what's up with you? The message was awful but she hit send and was rewarded with another reply.

Ridgeley wasn't actually her first name. It was her nickname. I never found out her real name because we only dated for about a month. I tried to tell you that back in the day but you didn't want to hear from me...

But back to your other question. I lived in Tucson for almost 14 years, then moved back to L.A. about a year ago. I don't know if I can sum up "what's up" in the past 15 years in a single message. Let me know if you want to get together.

Love always, Dave

Jane read the message four times in a row, then stood up to pace around her living room. "Love always" a second time? What did that mean? It meant they were cool, right? Dave was probably married so it couldn't mean more...

Oh my God, who cared? What was she thinking? Back to Ridgeley. Dave had only dated Ridgeley for a month? That was a surprise. A really nice one ... No, stop it, Jane! Who cares how long they dated? And Ridgeley was a nickname, but what the fuck was her real name then? And, seriously, even if they did only date for a month, how did her real name not come up?

This was a total dead end. So much for finding the painting easily. Now what was she going to tell Grandma Jeannie?

And Jane was back in touch with Dave. AHHH! Jane wasn't about to calm down and she knew it. There was way too much adrenaline in her system. Dave was back in her life! Wine wasn't going to help this time. Plus, she needed to think, not zone out.

Without much hesitation, she changed clothes, put on some running shoes, and hit the street. It'd been a long time since Jane worked out, but she had to get rid of energy somehow and the fresh air felt great. As she inhaled, she felt a crispness in her lungs she hadn't realized she'd missed. She ran until the burn felt bad. An exhausted, yet clear-headed Jane finally headed back inside for some wine and TV before bed.

* * *

Christine woke up in one of those moods where it seemed like she was walking through water. Everything was difficult this morning: brushing her teeth, getting dressed, wrangling the kids for school. She stopped herself from wishing Paul hadn't gone in early to work again and from picturing graphic scenarios of why. She didn't have time for that right now.

After dropping Lucy at kindergarten and Cameron at pre-K, and picking up an eco-unfriendly to-go cup of coffee, she pulled into the parking garage at her realty office. She glanced in the mirror and visibly sighed. She started to apply more make-up but quickly decided an additional layer of cosmetics could never cover up the dowdiness that emanated from within. With a breath of resignation, she exited her car.

"Hey Chris," she heard as she approached the elevator. The distinct voice belonged to young Frankie. Turning around, Christine replied, "'Morning Frankie," and a slow smile spread across her face. For some reason, the weighted feeling she had upon waking began to slowly evaporate.

Frankie looked like someone who shouldn't be named Frankie. Jane would have called him a Rex or an Ashton; she liked to give people the names she felt they looked like, regardless of what their names actually were. Frankie had an unassuming air and muscles for days. He was a nice, safe boy, but something about him whispered *danger* when he smiled with just that left corner of his mouth tipping up. With dark brown hair and a fashionably scruffy face, he couldn't be older than thirty, though Chris had never asked.

"I was wondering something. Obviously, I'm still pretty new here. I could use some strategies on how to build my client base. Would you be up for going to lunch sometime to discuss my approach?" And then the left corner of his mouth curled up into *that smile*.

"Sure. Yeah, of course," she replied without pause.

"Cool. I'll send you an invite."

Christine stifled a smile as they rode in silence up to their floor. Obviously, she was married and Frankie was so much her junior there was no way he saw her as a sexual being, unless he was into the whole few-extra-pounds-and-wrinkles thing. She scoffed at her own thoughts. Nonetheless, with the love slowly exiting from her own relationship, even the platonic attention of a male felt nice.

She muscled her way through work that day. A new listing kept her busy pulling comps in the area and doing general market analysis. Besides her morning run-in with Frankie, the highlight of her day was Jane's text filling her in on her progress with the painting. Looks like little sister had reconnected with Dave. Good. Christine always liked him.

That night, Chris found herself alone with her kids. Again. After dinner and some TV time, she put the kids to bed and went back downstairs to do laundry. *This is what I've become.* She was officially that past-her-prime wife who, despite having a full-time job, had to do everything at home while her aging-like-a-fine-wine husband spent hours away (likely with a hot soon-to-be divorcée). Realizing she was being dramatic, she focused on the task at hand.

As she pulled clothes out of the hamper, she pulled out a collared shirt of Paul's and stopped. Was that a fucking lipstick stain on the collar? It was faint, but it sure as hell looked like lipstick.

How cliché. And infuriating.

She called Jane. No answer. Fine. She took a picture of the collar and texted it to Paul with the caption *What's this?* She immediately saw 3 dots on her screen. *I have no idea.*

She wasn't sure what to think. It wasn't definitive proof of his infidelity, but she couldn't dismiss it either. Unsure what to do next, she poured herself a glass of chardonnay and watched some Real Housewives before going to bed.

As sleep overtook her, her dreams showed various scenarios involving her husband and Angela doing things they shouldn't, right in front of her. Paul making eye contact with Chris, feigning innocence as he was being mounted by the blonde. Christine looking in the mirror, seeing a reflection of her husband kissing Angela behind her. A courtroom scene where Chris was the defendant as Paul, the prosecutor, fondled Angela's naked breast. *Objection!*

After enough gut-wrenching scenes had played out, her mind did her a solid and took her in a very different direction. In this dream, her subconscious cast Frankie in the roll of much-too-young-but-still-legal sex object. In the work-based scenario, Frankie approached her asking for assistance with a PowerPoint he was working on for a new client. Once he was in her office, he closed the door and approached her slowly. He began caressing her neck with his lips and unbuttoning his own shirt. His mouth trailed down her cleavage as he shoved her dress over, revealing her breasts.

"I'd like to show you my power pointer," he whispered. Had she been awake, Christine would have laughed in his face, but this was a dream and, evidently, her subconscious didn't register cheesiness.

Frankie pulled her panties down gently and inserted two fingers inside of her.

"You have no idea how badly I want to fuck you," he said, his voice deep and hoarse, his fingers thrusting deep—

Christine woke in a sweat.

"You ok babe?" Paul murmured. She hadn't heard him come in.

"Yeah, I'm…good." She got out of bed and headed to the bathroom. Pulling her panties down to pee, she noticed she was soaking wet. Damn. She remembered the days when Paul would get her this ready. Maybe they should re-kindle that. But then, he'd have to actually be home and she knew *that* wasn't going to happen.

Christine crawled back into bed. Too tired for a full-on conversation with Paul about the (possible) lipstick stain, she allowed herself to fall back asleep until morning.

Once she had woken and fed the kids (Paul obviously already gone), Christine dropped them off at school and took a detour on the way to her office, driving by Paul's law firm to see if Angela's car was there. She couldn't help herself. By now she knew the woman drove a navy blue Lexus.

She wasn't even sure what information she hoped to get from this trip. After all, her husband *was* working on Angela's divorce case. However, the masochist in Chris had to know if the two were currently together.

As she pulled into the parking lot, she spotted the offending car immediately. Slow rolling past Paul's big office window, she half hoped to see them in some sort of compromising act so she could at least confront him. What she saw instead was her husband on his computer, Angela seated across from him.

It still made her feel sick. The beautiful woman was smiling endearingly. She really was gorgeous. Chris caught a glimpse of herself in the mirror and sighed. She gripped her steering wheel with unnecessary force and sped away from the scene. Paul's possible infidelity was one thing, but feeling like shit about herself was another. Before going to her office, she stopped back at home and packed a gym bag. She could start going on her lunch hour. At least it was something.

CHAPTER FOUR

Facebook had not led Jane to Ridgeley, but leading her to Dave was almost better. As much as she wanted to deny it, Grandma Jeannie's mission was already bringing her good things. She knew she had to keep going. Also, freelance volunteer detective work was kind of fun!

For the first time in a long time, Jane had a goal she felt motivated to achieve. Ridgeley may or may not still have Jane's painting, but even if she didn't, she was still the only one who might know where it ended up.

Ridgeley could be anywhere, doing anything. The only thing Jane knew about her for sure was that she was a talented artist. The failed Google attempt meant one of two things: either Ridgeley hadn't broken into the art world, or she was using a different name. Jane also knew that she would recognize Ridgeley's work in a heartbeat.

There was no other option. Pushing her anxiety down deep in her belly, Jane packed a backpack with a bottle of water and a light lunch, and then headed out to the Los Angeles Museum of Contemporary Art.

The odds of Ridgeley having made it big enough to be showing at the MOCA were almost zero. Art was a tough world to break into unless you were a legacy. Jane knew Ridgeley wasn't; she'd have heard about it in college. Professional art was, however, a very small world. The odds of two artists in the same medium knowing mutual people were very good, even if there were a few degrees of separation.

Artists were kind of like actors. Sure, it wasn't a guarantee that Kristen Wiig would know Anna Faris. But Kristen would know Amy Poehler from *SNL*, who would know Chris Pratt from *Parks and Rec*, who had been married to Anna Faris. Even if there wasn't such a direct connection, Kristen would likely know someone who knew someone who had met someone who knew Anna through a mutual friend, or whatever. Art worked the same way. Ridgeley definitely wasn't a Chris Pratt, but she might be the someone who knew someone. This would make her harder to find, but not impossible.

Ridgeley didn't create contemporary art per se, but Jane knew she pulled abstract features into her work, so to MOCA she went. Jane hated modern art so this would also be a relatively unpainful museum to begin with, one that may not pull at her soul as much as the others, asking it to re-awaken and rejoin their world. "Oh God," she said aloud at the floweriness of her own thought.

She re-focused.

If she saw a painting in a style similar to Ridgeley's Jane would have a jumping off point to search for Ridgeley's real name. She could take down the name of the painter and Google the crap out of that person, hoping to find other similar artists in a sort of backward tracking system. Jane began to feel like a pretty decent detective, and proudly wore a smirk of someone who was aiming to solve a mystery. Also, what's the worst that could happen? She'd spend a day among art, something that, though terrifying, was long overdue for Jane.

She hopped on the train toward downtown Los Angeles and managed to avoid the crazy man (there was always one) yelling about God and the End of Days by a clever use of earbuds.

The ride was long, giving her a chance to steel herself for the task ahead. There were a few things she hated about art museums. First, the art patrons. There was a dripping pretention and faux self-seriousness that so many aficionados brought with them. She could just hear the conversations now: "Sean? Why don't we do the LACMA on Sunday? Then we can picnic by the tar pits and perhaps catch a late afternoon matinee at the silent theater?" UGH. Go to a bar and complain about your life like the rest of America.

Next, the placards. *Oh God* the placards. They couldn't just say the names of the painting and the artist. Oh, no. They'd go on and on in diatribes of pure bullshit with words like "essence", "duality" and "reductive" peppered in so hard that any sane reader would be led to vomit, or at least sneeze in annoyance.

But the art itself. Jane had such a love-hate relationship with art. Because really, how could you love something if you didn't also hate it at least a little bit? She had just always loved art more than she hated it. Love: beautiful works with subtle features. Hate:

two-toned triangles pretending to be "abstract." Love: the feeling of belonging in the painting. Hate: the memory that she no longer painted. Love: the magical unifying quality of a brilliant piece, its on-lookers victims to the enchantment. Hate: everything she just thought. Ew.

When Jane finally arrived at the L.A. Museum of Contemporary Art trepidation set in. The MOCA. This was going to be tough. She hadn't been to the museum in years and even the last time she'd gone, she had struggled with taking some of the abstract modern art seriously. Some of it she understood, like the work of Tiana Farrawhey, whose ironic paintings portrayed complicated societal scenes with simple lines. But a lot of other artists' work fell victim to the "my five-year-old neighbor could have done that" point of view.

Open mind, she reminded herself. When she reached the front of the relatively small line (at least small compared to the line for the Broad—pronounced *BRODE*, because of course it was—across the street), the punk-inspired, 30-something Sydney woman behind the desk muttered something she couldn't understand. Assuming it related to buying a ticket, Jane thrust a twenty into the tiny intake hole and crossed her fingers the Sydney hadn't said something like, "Nice day, isn't it?"

She paid her $12 entrance fee and about-faced down the stairs, descending into either heaven or hell, she wasn't quite sure.

Bucking up, she exhaled. "Ready, break!" Jane whispered as she completed her 1-person huddle. She turned left and walked into the first room of the museum. An old and familiar feeling hit her like the lightest ton of bricks she had ever felt. Something— maybe the taste of regret?—crept into her mouth. She swallowed hard, remembering many afternoons lately spent on the couch that could've been spent here.

Taking everything in, Jane noticed the sleek walls, the sparsely placed paintings, and the handful of people milling about. Moving around the room, she peered at the first piece of "art." Here she saw what could only be described as a piece of black lacquer leaning against the wall. This was exactly what she had been afraid of. She read the placard. Yep. Some Gunther felt the piece reflected "the manic beat of New York paired with the laziness Los Angeles was attempting to re-attain with its gentrification."

When only a slight cough of derision escaped, she patted herself on the back for her restraint.

Making her way into various other rooms, she eventually saw a piece that made her smile. Recognizing the style of the artist immediately, she knew this was a Tiana Farrawhey. The painting portrayed the fish out of water in every way, and the whimsy of Tiana's work made the viewer smile while its depth of truth brought a tear to the viewer's eye. Tiana's use of color was inspiring.

This was art.

Before today Jane hadn't thought about her work in years. But seeing it here in this very museum reminded her of the love she had once felt for the artist. Tiana could reveal layers of the world that most people could recognize, though not necessarily define. Back before Ridgeley had taken art away from her Jane had once aspired to do the same.

She passed some Remys strolling along and heard phrases like "naiveté of an un-bruised child," and couldn't reign in her eye roll. She still hadn't seen what she was looking for. Nothing. Nothing at all reminded her of Ridgeley. Damn.

But just as she had that thought, she turned a corner and there it was.

It was a simple painting of mostly black, red, and yellow; the silhouette of a woman with a disproportionately-sized ass and breasts but with a smile so serene yet electric that it gave off the exact feel she was searching for. She approached the placard. *"Unabashed Woman", oil on canvas. Stephanie Serfshire, 2004.* She wrote down the name in her notebook, trying not to squeal at her first lead. This was certainly not a painting by Ridgeley. It would have had more mist and maybe something feline about it. However, there was something about it that evoked Ridgeley's style. Jane wasn't about to ignore the fact that she finally had a name to go on.

With a bit more gas in her tank, she continued her walk through the museum. As per always in contemporary art museums, there was, in fact, a two-toned triangle, a sculpture of lights, and a pile of something that looked like defecation. Art. Good to know that things hadn't changed that much since her last rodeo.

She exited the museum with more confidence than she had brought in. That wasn't so bad. Maybe she could check out the Broad across the street as well. It was mid-afternoon so the line had probably died down a bit…

Nope. It was half way down the block, and filled with more hipsters than she felt like dealing with. Time to regroup. She walked back to the train station, deep in thought. Today had been a success. Not only did she find a new lead, but she'd braved the big bad Museum of Contemporary Art. This giant leap in the right direction certainly had earned her a spot on the couch and big ass glass or three of wine tonight.

She would have had them anyway, but now it felt justified.

Once she arrived home, she poured herself a hefty glass of cab and grabbed a pad of paper and a pen. Still riding the high of her success, she decided to continue her investigation. Opening her computer, she looked up some more of Stephanie Serfshire's work. It was really good. Could Jane have been that good, had she stuck with it? *Was* she that good? She found herself drawing some of the curves of the painting she viewed, trying to match the style. Looking down, she answered her own question. Her scribbles were definitely not as good.

Envy crept in. God, Jane really could have become something if it hadn't been for Ridgeley. But no, that wasn't true. Ridgeley hadn't actually made any decisions for Jane. She wasn't the one who quit art and changed majors.

Jesus Christ. Something snapped into place, something Chris and Elle and a whole lot of people throughout the years had been telling her. Ridgeley hadn't taken art away from her. *Oh God,* Ridgeley hadn't taken Dave away from her either. She had left them both. She had let her jealousy of Ridgeley destroy her fragile ego and she had ditched the two things most important to her. Elle's constant talks about how kids at the center blamed their parents for their own misfortunes sank a level deeper. Jane had been doing the exact same thing.

As painful as this realization was, it was probably a good one to have. Even if it was 15 years too late.

Taking no more time for self-reflection, she picked up her phone and hit her Facebook Messenger app to contact Dave. She had never owed anyone this big of an apology. Needing to dissipate some energy, she scribbled some doodles on the notepad before typing out her message.

Dave. Oh my God. I'm so sorry, she sent without explanation.

He responded immediately. *Oh Jane. It's ok. I forgave you years ago.*

Wow. She had truly been the only one to believe her own bullshit.

I went to a museum today Dave. And it was terrible. And amazing. And I miss you.

Janey, I've missed you for 15 years. He quickly added, *I mean, not constantly. I'm not a psychopath.*

Something in Dave's tone released her tension and she laughed out loud.

Dave continued. *What inspired you to go to the museum?*

The Ridgeley mission. I need to find this painting for my grandma. It's a whole thing. Hey, what's your daughter's name?

Daughter? What are you talking about?

That gave Jane pause, but he responded before she could answer.

Do you mean the girl in my Facebook pic? Janey, that's Gracie's kid. My niece, Bella.

Gracie! Jane had only met Dave's sister once, but they had gotten along famously. Of course the girl was Gracie's daughter; they looked exactly alike. Relief washed over Jane, but why? It's not like she and Dave were a thing.

More scribbling. Emboldened, she responded.

What are you doing right now? Let's talk.

She froze in ecstatic fear as she awaited his response. She'd been terrified to meet up with Dave. After over a decade of silence, it was too much at once. But a phone call might work.

What's your number? he replied.

Oh my God. She sent it. Seconds later, her phone rang.

"Hello?" Jane said, as if she didn't know who it was.

She totally knew who it was.

"Janey, Janey." Oh God, just hearing his voice sent shivers down her spine. She loved when he called her Janey. She loved his voice, that sultry baritone that sent goosebumps down her arms. The familiarity made it seem impossible that so many years had passed since she last heard it.

"Holy shit Dave. I…I can't even believe this." As she braced herself for hours of conversation, the line went silent. "H-hello?"

She looked down at her phone. Dead.

Nooooo! Taking her pen, she tore out her frustration on the page.

Needing to make sure he knew she wasn't running away again, she rushed back to her computer, frantically typing. *My phone died! I promise I didn't hang up!* Did that sound too desperate? No, just desperate enough. She wanted to bang her head on the table.

She waited in panic until his reply popped up. *No worries, Janey. Again, let me know if you want to meet up sometime. Miss your face :)*

She slumped in relief. Whew. Grabbing her wine, she looked down at her paper. Oh my God. An outline of her own frustrated face. And it wasn't bad. For the first time in 15 years, she had created art. Doodles counted. She snapped a shot and sent it to Christine. Downing her wine, she poured herself another much, much deserved glass.

* * *

Elle woke to more messages in her Buzz inbox. She'd sent out a few texts recently, but felt uninspired after her encounter with Owen. As she threw off her covers and pulled herself out of bed, she opened each one. After sifting through the "How is your day going?" messages, she stumbled upon something interesting.

Your "sexy selfie" is a bit redundant, isn't it, considering the photo directly above it?

Hmm. Elle perused her own profile. The photo she had facetiously titled "sexy selfie" was anything but. It was a purposefully unflattering photo of her right before going to bed, meant to off-set the filtered and floral headband shots of other women. She scrolled up. The pic he was referring to as the original sexy photo was an equally ridiculous shot of Elle and Jane at KC's making over-the-top duck faces as their high-score on PhotoHunt featured heavily in the background. To Elle, it was much more important to display personality in her profile rather than overly touched-up pictures of herself in a dress she'd never wear in real life.

This fellow had seemed to understand her angle, which piqued her interest.

Tapping on his profile, she read that he was Irish, so he had automatic points for the accent. He had written very little about himself (extra points) but what he had written had charm. "Oh God. I should have added a shirtless photo of me holding a tiger. I've made a horrible mistake," his profile concluded, which made Elle smile. As she reviewed his content, she looked at her list. He definitely seemed fun. But was this a person who wanted a relationship and kids? Nothing in his profile indicated this either way. Time to be bold.

I'm going to cut to the quick. Are you looking for a relationship? And do you want kids? I mean, not necessarily with me, we're strangers. Send.

She waited a few hours—ok maybe it just *felt* like hours—for a response she wasn't sure she'd get. Then, her phone pinged.

Damn, Elle. I appreciate the directness. I do want a relationship and kids, and while I know we're strangers, I'm not yet ruling you out as the potential mother.

Elle laughed. This guy was either awesome or crazy. Thus far he was checking items off her list nicely. She pivoted back to lighter conversation, starting with a hard Cranberries reference.

So, Ireland? Isn't that where everyone's fighting, with their tanks, and their bombs, and their bombs, and their guns?

Nah. It's all in your heee-aaad, in your heeee-aaaad. An equally strong Cranberrries reference. Nice.

Elle felt a tightening in her stomach. Could that be excitement? She pulled on her leather jacket and squeezed her phone before pocketing it and heading for work.

As she walked into the center Elle was immediately bombarded with shouting teens.

"Hey Miss Elle!"

"Miss E!"

"Damn Elle, looking good."

At that one she stopped.

"Skye, we've talked about this."

Skye, a 14-year-old who identified as male, winked back impishly and Elle couldn't help but crack a half smile. The center was multifunctional. It served as a shelter for teens who had nowhere else to go, as well as a counseling center. They offered crisis counseling to kids in acute situations, as well as ongoing therapy, which was where Elle came in. The kids she helped didn't necessarily live at the center, but they tended to hang out there. She had weekly clients and open drop-in hours. Beyond direct therapy, she also ran some talk groups and some of the activities the center offered, like basketball. As she prepped for her first session with a lesbian teen who had recently come out to her parents, she checked her phone a final time. Yes! There was another message from Ireland! The emoji made her smile as she turned off her phone and transitioned into therapist mode.

Elle's morning sessions flew by and her afternoon was peppered with witty banter with her new Irish Beau. The hits kept on coming; he was delightfully funny and handsome to boot. She briefly allowed herself to wonder what his fatal flaw might be. There had to be one—why else would he be on a dating app? Sure, she was too but she *knew* what her flaws were! Could he be catfishing her? Maybe he had an intolerably annoying voice? What if he was married? She couldn't stop the flaw-hunting but it definitely slowed as their conversation got deeper. They started talking about things like college, what they were like growing up. By the end of the night, they were on to past relationships and what they wanted from their next. He didn't even give the typical straight-guy "that's hot" comment when she said she was bisexual. Elle was excited by this one; it felt like he might have potential. Obviously it was too soon to tell. But maybe.

The next day went by in a similar fashion and that night when Elle went over to Jane's to get an update on the Great Painting Mystery, Jane immediately busted her for glancing at her phone far too frequently.

"What the fuck is going on?" Jane asked the fourth time Elle "just wanted to see what time it was."

"Nothing. Don't make a big deal about it."

Jane stared back. "Nobody cares about the time that much. What. Is. Up."

"I'm talking to a guy. He's... I don't know. He's cool so far."

"He's cool so far. Ever the one for details," Jane snarked back.

"Fine. He's funny, and he's... I don't know what else. I like him. He's got potential."

"Let me see your phone or I'll keep grilling you."

With a slight eye-roll, Elle handed her phone over. As she did so, she gasped. "*What* is on your hands?"

Jane looked down at her smudged-up digits. "Oh. Pencil." She paused when Elle gave her a cheesy grin. "What?"

"Jane, have you been drawing?"

"What's the big deal? I've just been doodling a bit."

"Uh huh." The competition of who could remain the chilliest continued. "You've been drawing and you didn't say anything."

"Whatever. You've been talking to a guy and you didn't say anything." With that, Jane turned to Elle's phone.

It took a good 5 minutes for her to get through the messages that had begun only the day before. "Holy shit-show Elle, this dude is legit. I say go for it."

Elle almost fell out of her chair in relief. She didn't need her best friend's approval, but it definitely felt nice to get it.

Later that night, Ireland asked Elle when he could see her. Elle started. Huh. They hadn't made any official plans yet. She looked at her calendar and begrudgingly reviewed her work-related conflicts over the next few days. *Can we do Thursday?*

I cannot wait, you fantastic creature. Oh boy. Thursday could not come fast enough.

Elle went to bed that night on a cloud of euphoria. What if this was it? And Irish genes for her future little one wouldn't be so bad. They'd have an adorable little redheaded lass with an accent! Oh, and they'd get both a flat in Dublin and a country cottage, so her daughter could experience city life and the green rolling hills. Maybe they could be sheep herders! How hard could that be? And then Elle could learn to knit and make cool, cozy sweaters from her own sheep and maybe even start a clothing line. But what would she call it?—

Elle shook her head. Jesus, she needed to pump the brakes.

Thursday at work was an absolute blur. Elle was usually completely checked-in at the center, available to any of the teens who needed it. Today, not so much. Not wanting to provide sub-par services, she decided to complete long overdue paperwork rather than have client drop-in time.

After lunch, she felt suddenly nauseous. This feeling was unfamiliar. She texted Jane. *I think I have anxiety.*

Get over it. The short and unsweet hype message was enough. Elle powered through the rest of her day and went on a post-work walk to calm her nerves.

Once home, she showered and got ready. Ireland was going to meet her at her apartment. Normally she'd scoff at anyone who gave their personal address to a complete stranger for a first date, but he didn't feel like a stranger to her. They already had a bond, and she was optimistic it was one that could last. She was putting the finishing touches on her barely-there-but-enough-to-make-her-look-sexy makeup when her phone buzzed with a message.

10 minutes until I see your gorgeous face.

Like an excited teenager, she sat in silence, waiting for her apartment's buzzer to sound. Once it did, she leaped off of her sofa and threw on her jacket, ready to head out.

Opening the front door, she and Ireland looked at each other and sparks filled the air. Without a word, they embraced in a gentle but passionate kiss. *Fuck yes!*

Head spinning, Elle took a half step-back without breaking their embrace and took a few seconds to look deeply into the eyes of the man she already knew.

"Hey," she said weakly through thick emotions.

"Hi there, beautiful," he responded, pecking her on the cheek. He brought a bottle of wine, and she allowed him to step in over to her coffee table to set it down. God. Even the way he *walked* was sexy.

This was good. Ireland looked around her apartment, took her hands, and said, "Ay, ya fuckin' gaff's got … ??????…ta liffin." Or something like that.

"What?" Elle responded. "I only understood a few words of that." He laughed and they stepped back out her door into the streets of Los Angeles to wander.

They held hands as they strolled. Ireland spoke at rapid-fire speed for a few minutes straight, pausing only enough for Elle to interject with "What?" After every "can you talk a little slower? I can't really understand you," he would respond by repeating whatever he'd said, then continuing full speed ahead.

She felt like she was in the movie *Snatch*, only there were no subtitles.

Twenty minutes later they arrived at a park and sat at the overlook. Maybe being able to see his lips as he spoke would help her understand him. She hoped.

"Ay, look at da,'" he began. "Mi brodda Ian wu da ha … ???????"
He continued for at least 3 minutes.

Watching his lips did *not* help.

Elle's previous butterflies went back in their cocoons. She had
no fucking clue what this guy was saying, and he was not taking her
blatant cues to slow down or engage with her at all.

Ireland reached over to kiss her passionately but Elle hesitated.

"Ah, ya den't like tha. Some-in happ'nd." That she understood
and relief overcame her as she realized he had noticed her subtle
body language. This was salvageable; he was probably just overcome
with nerves. Lord knew she was.

"You're talking really fast and it's kind of intense."

"Ah, ok," he started, which was a positive sign. And then he
was off again, "Bu I jus've been told tha all mi life, mi brodda Ian
says … shirt … Bible … th' fuckin' Universe …"

Well, fuck. She had certainly never imagined Prince Charming
as Guy Ritchie.

She was able to pull enough content from what he said to
understand his rapid and frequent speech was not just a result of
nerves; this was just how he talked. And damn, did he talk a lot.
After his forty-eighth monologue about only Dolores O'Riordan
knew what, a deflated Elle suggested they end their evening. Such
a bummer.

The walk back to Elle's was awkward at best. It was a mix of
silence and unintelligible Irish speeches. She looked forward to the
bottle of wine that was sitting, waiting in her apartment, which she'd
now be drinking alone. Fuck it, she'd have whiskey.

She was not looking forward to updating Jane, who had been
so optimistic for her on this outcome.

At her door, Ireland took one look at her face and smiled ruefully. "Ah, ay've gon un fuuhkt this up, aven't aye?"

"It's not like that. I just feel like we're not quite a match," she responded, trying to let him down softly. God he was gorgeous, but she couldn't make babies with someone she couldn't even talk to. Her redheaded daughter would be a full-time translator, English to English. And she'd only be translating for him, because Elle couldn't get a word in edgewise! No way. Disappointing as it was, this was done.

As she closed the door, her phone binged with a text from Jane.

Soo... Are you pregnant yet?

Fuck. Everything. It hurt that her balloon-full of potential had so suddenly popped. Next time, she'd have to keep her emotions a bit more in check. App dating wasn't like regular dating where the person already had context in your life, like mutual friends. Ireland had been a stranger and she'd allowed herself to be caught up in a fairytale. Why couldn't she just meet someone in real life? Jane reminded her that that wasn't a thing anymore. Resigned, she settled in to the Real Housewives of Wherever. As she poured herself a glass of whiskey, Elle took out her list and added a bullet point:

Can have a two-way conversation.

* * *

Christine was filling up her coffee cup in the company breakroom when she heard Frankie's voice behind her. Her stomach dropped a bit in a way she wasn't entirely ok with. Turning around, she noticed Frankie's jaw tighten when he caught her neckline. Her blouse had slipped down slightly farther than she had planned, though even in its current position it was hardly scandalous. Was he attracted to her? That seemed impossible, but in her current state of mind she wasn't mad about it.

"Hey you," he said.

"Hey you back." Ugh. That was awful. She barely avoided cringing visibly.

"How's your workload these days? You still the queen of selling houses?"

She laughed. Too hard. But he didn't seem to notice? "Oh, I'm doing alright. I'm just about to close out a listing, and I've got a property in escrow."

"Very impressive." He flashed *that* smile. Chris stifled a gulp. *Play it cool.*

"Thanks," she replied. *Not bad.*

"I like your shirt by the way. It looks really nice on you," he added, maintaining eye contact so as not to look at her breasts? God, she hoped. Christine finally pulled her inner confidence to the surface.

"I appreciate that, Frankie. Very much." She cocked her head to the side and bit her lip gently. It had the desired effect; Frankie's eyes darkened and his smile grew. *Yes!*

"Are you still up for grabbing lunch soon?" Frankie asked nonchalantly.

"Sure. How about tomorrow?" Christine cooed back. Wait, what? Cooing? What was *that* about? Her cool was officially gone, but it didn't matter. It was on with Frankie. *Lunch! Lunch* was on. Nothing more. He was new to the office and she, after all, was the *queen* of real estate. He had said it himself! The kid needed a mentor. And that she could do.

She continued her day, a bit brighter for the run-in, and around lunch time she grabbed her work-out bag and headed to the gym. This was a routine she had adopted lately, and results were beginning to show. Not that Paul had noticed. Had Frankie? *Who cares!* She wasn't working out for anyone else; she was doing it for herself.

As she entered the gym, a trainer greeted her. Chris smiled, realizing she was such a regular that the staff knew her name. Her gym was her very own *Cheers*!

She stepped onto the elliptical machine, and her body easily fell into motion. Breathing steadily, she leaned in to the work-out. What the hell was up with her marriage? She moved a little faster, pumping her arms and legs rhythmically with the machine. Was Paul really cheating? She turned the machine up a level. Her kids. God, had her kids noticed anything going on with Mommy and Daddy? Panting. Moving harder. The cadence was her therapy. Pain rose but she moved through it. 30 minutes in, she glanced at the machine and hit "cool down." With a clearer head and a clear cache of energy, she smiled. Maybe it would all be ok.

Chris showered and re-dressed for work. Grabbing a smoothie from the snack bar, the same trainer hollered out, "See you tomorrow, Chris."

Turning to respond, Chris paused. "Actually, you won't. I'm having lunch with a … colleague."

Her head clouded. Should she cancel on Frankie? But why? Lunch was the most innocent meal of the day. Dinner implied a date and breakfast implied an affair. She could cheat on her self-care for one day. After all, that was *all* she'd be cheating on.

CHAPTER FIVE

Jane opened her laptop and re-typed in the name Stephanie Serf-shire. This time she wasn't looking for her art; she was looking for clues. Apparently, Stephanie had recently moved from L.A. to New York. How geographically inconvenient. However, fellow artist Angela Ashbury was frequently paired with Stephanie in articles and blogs. Angela was evidently an art teacher who had worked with both Stephanie and Tiana Farrawhey, meaning she was legit. She might even have ties to Ridgeley.

Angela didn't have her own wiki-page, but seeing as how her students all spent some time in Los Angeles, Jane assumed Angela was here as well. Jane continued scouring the web for information until she hit the jackpot. Not only was Angela local, but she held drop-in classes every Wednesday evening on charcoal technique. With a glimmer of a spark snaking through her belly, Jane marked her calendar for next Wednesday and called Chris.

"Guess what the fuck I've been up to?" she practically yelled when her big sis picked up the phone.

"Lucy! Hang on honey," Chris yelled to her five-year-old daughter, then sighed. "Sorry. What have you been up to?"

"I went to a goddamn museum and I *might* have found a link to Ridgeley!" Jane paused for the roar of applause that was sure to follow.

"That's great," Chris offered, disappointingly.

Something was off. "What's up with you?" Jane asked.

"Nothing. I'm happy for you. Sorry, I'm just dealing with the kids. Can we talk later?"

"Of course."

"Lucy, hang on!" Chris yelled before hanging up.

Hmm. Jane would have to check back in when Chris was in more of a talking mood. She poured herself a glass of wine and logged in to Facebook. Her heart jumped as she saw she had a message from Dave.

Hey you. Just checking in. Simple, and so Dave.

Jane wrote back, telling him that she'd be going to an art class to speak with Angela.

Dave responded quickly. Was the man always online? *That sounds awesome! I'm glad to see you're still doing art stuff.*

I mean, I wouldn't say I'm still doing art stuff. Really I'm just trying to find an old painting. She filled him in about Grandma Jeannie, the painting, and Jane's search. Toward the end of her explanation, Jane went deep. *I blamed Ridgeley for everything. And honestly, the more I look at, the less impact she actually had on me. It was all in my head. People tried to tell me back then but I didn't believe them.* Send.

She added, *Ever get to a point in life where you realize you're the cause of all your bullshit?*

Three dots appeared. Then deleted. Then appeared again.

Finally, Dave answered. *Yes.*

Hmm. What were his regrets?

Dave's affirmative reply was all she needed to muster up some courage. Jane missed her friend and she wanted to see him. He had floated the idea of meeting up twice already, but a terrified Jane had shirked the invites. What was her problem?

Fear had run enough of her life. Plus, this man used to be her best friend. *Want to grab some coffee sometime soon?* Before she could talk herself out of it, she hit send.

How about Saturday? Dave offered. And it was set.

* * *

Chris might as well be a single parent. After working all day she was now doing Second Shift and getting the kids fed, helping them put away their toys, directing their bedtime routine, and tucking them in. Between that and the vacuuming, dusting, and scouring the kitchen of whatever sticky thing Cameron had managed to spread all over the place, she was exhausted and, as usual, was in bed before Paul was home from work. Again.

Her dreams that night again oscillated between heart-wrenching scenes involving her husband and his potential mistress, and naughtiness with Frankie. Upon waking, she was sad, yet unsurprised, to see that Paul was already gone. Mixed emotions fueled her morning routine, creating an intensity and dedication she usually lacked. After putting on her make-up, she looked critically at her reflection in the full-length mirror, expecting to find the usual flaws.

But instead she was shocked. Was her stomach looking a little less flabby? And her thighs looked tighter too. She hadn't been working out for long but she could see a little improvement. Without meaning to, she had also been extra careful with her hair and makeup.

For the first time in a long time, Christine felt sexy.

Her kids seemed to recognize her uplifted spirits as well. "Mama, you pretty!" Cameron stated in that matter-of-fact way that 4-year-olds have.

"Thank you, sweetheart," she replied. It felt nice to be noticed, even if it was just by her baby. Now if only her husband was home to appreciate her.

She went to work and got lost in the world of real-estate. Come noon, Christine gave herself a quick mirror check and walked toward Frankie's cubicle for their lunch meeting. Such a darling young man, still working in a cubicle. Her mini-makeover had done wonders for her self-confidence. Noting her Mrs. Robinson-level swag, she tried to tone it down. But hey, at least she wasn't in a frump-slump.

Flinging her jacket over her right shoulder, Christine leaned against the wall of Frankie's cubicle. A moment of panic set in as she realized she may look like a fool. But any nervousness was set aside the moment Frankie looked up at her and appeared to lose his ability to speak.

Evidently, her look was effective.

"Wow. You look ... nice," he managed.

Christine bit her cheek so as not to let on how elated the

comment made her. The idea of making this twenty-something young thing squirm made her wetter than a slip-and-slide.

"Thanks Frankie. Shall we?" Mustering her best Mae West, Christine turned slowly away from him to give him the full impact of her womanly curves and sauntered toward the door. She was really over-doing this. Jane would be laughing her ass off, but Frankie seemed to have a different reaction. She thought she saw him adjust himself slightly and felt giddy. *She* had done that to him!

Ok, time to rein it in. If she was going to play like she was doing nothing wrong, she had better do nothing wrong. While it was fun to get the self-confidence boost, Frankie was a sweet kid. She didn't need to use him that way. Chris surreptitiously wiped off her lipstick, buttoned the top button on her blouse, and made herself promise she'd act like a professional.

Frankie offered to drive to a diner nearby. In the car on the way over, he thanked Christine for taking the time to meet with him. He synched his phone with the car stereo and REO Speedwagon started playing. Well, this was a surprise.

"No way," Christine said.

"No seriously, I admire you professionally."

"I meant the music."

"Oh, Speedwagon is classic. My parents listened to them when I was a kid."

That was the reality check she needed; technically, she could be Frankie's mom. With her lady boner officially gone, Christine transitioned into business mode.

Lunch was decent and she allowed Frankie to pick her brain about how to best market small houses that were neither tear-downs nor move-in ready. Chris had fifteen years' worth of experience in the real estate business and was always happy when her knowledge could help out a colleague. Especially one with such delicious muscles and an endearing smile ... *Nope, stop that. He needs a mentor, not a Sugar Mama.* Still, it was hard not to notice the way his eyes lit up when he got excited, or the way his mouth curled up when he smiled.

That evening, surprisingly, Paul was home at a decent time. He'd even brought home take-out to give her a much-needed break from cooking. Chris felt a pang of guilt. He was trying. Was she? She'd done nothing wrong; having thoughts about another man weren't the same as acting on them.

"How was your day, babe?" Paul asked.

"It was good," she offered. Should she tell Paul about Frankie? Why not? She had nothing to hide. "I had lunch with a new colleague, Frankie. He asked to pick my brain."

"That's nice of you, helping out the new guy. How'd it go?"

"It was fine. He's a young one, pretty new to the business. I feel like I helped him."

"That's great," Paul replied. "I'm sure he appreciated it."

See? Nothing to feel bad about here. And, more than that, she and Paul were actually talking!

"Thanks. I think he did. He called me the queen of real estate."

"You are. You're the queen of *this* real estate, that's for sure." Was that an actual compliment? Hot damn.

"This is nice. We haven't chatted in a while," she responded, offering the metaphorical olive branch in outstretched hand.

"It is." Paul stood up and kissed her on the cheek before filling up his wine. Affection! See, their marriage was fine. They were communicating. She had been open about Frankie, because why wouldn't she be? Good. They were both focused on what was important: their family. Keeping the conversation going, Chris piped back up.

"How was work for you?" she returned the question.

Paul's shoulder's tensed visibly. "Good. Stressful. Things are crazy, but I'm, you know, handling it."

"Oh yeah. Stressful how?" *Talk to me, Paul.*

"Just … clients. You know." He took a big gulp of wine. "I don't really want to talk about it."

"You don't think it'd help to talk about it with me? Maybe I can help you feel less stressed."

Paul sighed. "No, you really can't. And you know I can't discuss clients' confidential information, so please stop asking."

Wow, what a slap in the face. Christine's mind went back to Angela. She was a client. Certainly Paul would feel stressed if he had a "conflict of interest", say, fucking his client. And if he wasn't, if everything was fine, then why had he shut the conversation down so hard? She'd told him about Frankie, which was innocent. If he had nothing to hide, why was he hiding?

Chris felt gross and her throat clenched up. How could she confront Paul about what was going on? Whenever she put on a full-court press, Paul shut down. He'd always been that way. When faced with confrontation, he'd bottle his emotions instead of face them.

Chris wasn't interested in a night of terse silence; she decided to shelve the whole thing. Even though it killed her not to know what was really going on, time would eventually reveal all secrets. At that point she could make a decision.

After dinner, Paul got the kids ready for bed as Christine

enjoyed a glass of wine on the couch. Suddenly her phone buzzed. She looked at it and her stomach dropped an inch.

It was Frankie.

I just wanted to thank you again for our lunch. It was really helpful. Also, if you don't mind my saying so, you looked great. Hope that doesn't come off too creepy, lol. Thanks again!

The text was totally inappropriate, yet it made Christine bite her lip with excitement. Was replying wrong? Her loving (but possibly cheating) husband was currently tucking in their children. It wasn't cheating, but surely texting with Frankie was not ok.

But she was going to do it anyway.

You're very welcome, and thank you :) There. That wasn't all bad. No court of law would find her guilty of cheating with that response. She and Paul had been together for so long, what was a bit of harmless texting anyway?

As Christine sat on the couch, she twirled her wineglass. How the fuck had her marriage come to this when their relationship had started so sweetly? As a college junior at UCLA, Christine Baker decided to be wing-girl for her bestie Stephanie at a Halloween party. Never one to feel fully comfortable letting her slut flag fly with her costume choice, she threw together a last-minute costume of Carmen Sandiego. Steph, on the other hand, went with an *I Dream of Jeannie*-style genie, with tiny boy shorts under sheer harem pants and a crop top that made a bra look conservative.

"Well done," Christine said as she sized up her friend. "You look hot as hell. Ty Grojan won't know what hit him." Steph had the *biggest* crush on the big man on campus. "I hope you're good with Ty wanting your body more than your mind, at least tonight."

"Oh girl, I'm good with it," Stephanie replied as a huge grin spread across her face.

As they approached the house, Christine protested. "You did not tell me Ty lived in a frat house."

"Of course I didn't. You wouldn't have come!" Steph replied, accurately. Christine had been in her thirties since she was eighteen, and truly didn't see the point in fraternizing with frat boys, or going to college parties in general. She groaned audibly, in too deep to turn back now.

Walking in the front door, a wall of sweat and Busch Lite hit Chris's olfactory nerves like a ton of bricks. She had to hold back a dry heave. Ew. Frat guys were gross.

Mindful of her duties as wing-girl, they did a lap around the room, searching for Ty. And there he was, dressed as Marky Mark from his Calvin Klein ads wearing only tighty-whites. He'd cleverly added a sign that read "Marky Mark." You know, just in case it wasn't obvious.

Chris rolled her eyes. Stephanie could do better, truly. But making mistakes was what college was about, wasn't it? Christine gently nudged her friend toward her crush. After the obligatory introductions, Christine gave the potential lovebirds some space. It was too early to bail on the party, as there was still a fifty-fifty chance this evening would end in tears for Steph. She was a bit of a dramatic, and Chris had to see if she'd need a shoulder to cry on.

The best way to pass time, she decided, was to have a few beers. Then a few more. Then maybe hit the dance floor. After all, "The Thong Song" was playing. Who could resist that "thong-thong-thong-thong-thong"?

She was killing her solo during the key change when she slipped and bumped into a couple, causing the girl to spill her drink all over a drunken Tarzan. "What the fuck, bitch?" drunk Tarzan threatened Chris, glaring at her sprawled on the floor.

"Sorry," she said, getting to her feet.

"Sorry doesn't fix my fucking costume," drunk Tarzan said as he towered over her menacingly. What the fuck was happening?

Just then, a sweet and mostly sober Mr. Potato Head jumped in between them.

"Hey Tarzan, it was an accident. Nobody likes to watch a big muscular dude like you pick on a cute little lady, ok? Why don't you guys grab another drink and chill out. You mind getting him another drink?" he said to Tarzan's woman. "Great costumes by the way."

Confused, drunk Tarzan and his date agreed that another drink was their best option and walked toward the kitchen.

Mr. Potato Head turned to Christine. "You ok?" he asked genuinely.

And just like that, she burst into tears.

"Thank you. Thank you so much. Oh God, what's wrong with me? I'm not a crier. I'm not. I'm not a crier-drunk. And I'm not usually the drunk. I'm the taker-carer of drunks. I swear. Oh God, shut up Christine." She took a deep breath. "Thank you."

"You're very welcome. I'm Paul, also a taker-carer. It's nice to meet you."

She hugged him. Not her usual M.O. but he had just done her a solid in a sea of strangers. Surely that was a hug-worthy, right?

"Let me get you a water," he added, handing her a sealed bottle from a table nearby.

Paul and Christine talked for a while outside. As she sobered up, her word vomit dried up too. She learned that he was pre-law, and from the Mid-West, and that he also hadn't wanted to come to the party this evening.

Around midnight Christine felt good enough to do a final check on Stephanie and, if she was ok, head out. She walked through the house, her shoes sticking to the floor with every step, and spotted her friend and Ty ravenously kissing. Smiling, she shouted out, "Steph I'm leaving." Her friend gave her a thumbs-up without breaking make-out. The girl had skills.

She went to thank Paul for babysitting her, but he offered to walk her home. "Nothing creepy, I swear. I'd just like to make sure you get home safe." He was so earnest. Christine allowed the sweetness of him to sink in.

It was a good feeling.

On the walk home, Paul walked street-side to keep Chris away from traffic. This was one of those chivalrous things that could be perceived as anti-feminist, but it would only be annoying from someone putting on airs. Paul reeked of genuineness. At her house, Paul said good-night and paused. He appeared to be manning up to ask for her number, but she didn't need him to be brave. He'd clearly earned it so she gave it freely.

They looked at each other, both not wanting to go, but not sure what else to say. In another out of character move, Christine wrapped her arms around Paul, looked him dead in the eyes, then leaned in and kissed him.

Oh God. His lips! They were soft and firm at the same time, sweet and electric. She'd never kissed such perfect lips before. She could kiss them for all eternity!

Finally, Paul paused from the kiss to speak. "When can I see you again?" he whispered in her ear.

"Tomorrow," she whispered back.

Chris hadn't realized her kiss with Paul that night would be her last first kiss, but it was. And for the longest time, she'd been glad of that. Now, twenty years later, she shook her head as she took a long sip of her drink. The truth was, they had both been so young when they got together and couples sometimes outgrow each other. Like all relationships, they'd had their ups and downs but they'd always managed to pull through. Never before had they had a lull last as long as the current one. They'd built a solid and loving relationship and birthed two amazing children who they both adored. But solid wasn't sexy and it wasn't fun.

If Christine was being really honest, she could see her own contributions to the current state of the relationship. She also wasn't communicating her thoughts and feelings. And why wasn't she? She used to share everything with Paul. How many times had they stayed up late into the night, chatting about their day, their goals, or even just their thoughts about some crappy TV show they were watching? Where had that intimacy gone?

And speaking of intimacy, when was the last time they'd had sex? Chris fancied herself quite the sexual being, but there had been times recently where she'd shut Paul down when he'd come onto her. That couldn't have been good for his self-esteem. She just hadn't been in the mood. She hadn't felt attractive, which makes it difficult to feel sexy or crave sex. But lately, with all the gym time she'd been putting in, Chris was feeling a bit better about herself. Paul, however, hadn't seemed to notice the transformation.

Well. She'd just have to *make* him notice.

With that, she sauntered up the stairs. She didn't have to take this one lying down. Or better yet, maybe she and Paul *should* be laying down. Unbuttoning her shirt, she slipped it off her shoulders as she entered the bedroom. Things were about to heat up, and hopefully thaw the cold center of their marriage.

As she crawled into bed, reaching under the covers to please her husband, she leaned in to kiss him. But she stopped herself before she started—Paul was sound asleep.

Chris could still work with that. She'd seen enough R rated movies to realize he'd love for her to wake him up with her hands and mouth. She started to reach for him again…

And then he snored. He really had been exhausted lately. Perhaps she should let him get some much-needed rest.

Realizing the best move she could make for her marriage was to allow the man to sleep, Chris settled in to read a book. Oh, well. They had made some strides tonight toward communicating better. Things would be fine.

And then her phone pinged. Frankie. *I can't wait to see you tomorrow.*

Fuck. That was a nice message to get.

* * *

Elle was excited to get to work. After the Ireland fiasco she was grateful for the opportunity to take her mind off of herself and put it toward helping others.

Her first appointment was with a teen she hadn't worked with before. Maria was a 16-year-old bisexual female. She lived at home with her mom who tried to be supportive but didn't understand her daughter's sexuality. She thought it was a phase. Elle tried not to roll her eyes. They always thought it was a phase.

Maria was pregnant. Of course, her boyfriend had left as soon as he found out. So here she was, sixteen, pregnant, and single. Maria was adamant that she wanted to keep her baby. This made Elle's job easier, as her client had already come to her own answer to this very big question. But poor Maria was heartbroken and terrified. Dark hair loose, green eyes crying, Maria spoke. "I'm so confused about everything. I mean, I know I want the baby. I can't imagine abortion or adoption. And I know this wasn't what we planned, but I thought he loved me. How could Ethan leave so easily? I just don't know what I'm doing."

"I know girl. But most people don't know what they're doing. We're all just winging it day by day. I know it doesn't seem like it. There are plenty of people you look at and think, 'Man, they've got it all figured out.' But I promise you, they're just as full of self-doubt as you are at this moment." Elle reached out and took Maria's hand. "You're going to be ok. Ethan left and that sucks, but you've still got people who are here to support you."

Maria's head popped up. "That's what my mom said. She said I'll be fine, that I've got her, and this center, and you."

Grateful for Maria's mom's support, Elle smiled. "There, you see? I know you didn't plan this. But you're not alone. You're a smart, brave woman. You can do this."

Maria gave a watery laugh. "I'm gonna be a single mom. Like my mom. Shit."

She talked Maria through the rest of the hour, and the session ended with Elle giving her information on some resources that helped new mothers. They set up weekly appointments going forward. Maria seemed a little lighter on her feet as she left Elle's office.

Truly believing the girl would be fine, Elle reflected. If this teenager could raise a baby on her own, why the hell couldn't she? Elle's mom had been a single mom too, and she'd turned out fine. Maybe having a second parent for a baby wasn't as important as she'd been making it. Had Elle been going about this all wrong? She really would rather have a partner to help, but maybe…just maybe…if she didn't find one, she could still be a mom. As she'd told Maria, plenty of women raised kids as single moms. Hell, even some married women were practically single moms when you looked at how little their husbands did. If Elle didn't find a good man—or woman—then maybe she should just have a baby on her own.

Not yet though! For now, she still planned to make it work the old-fashioned way.

CHAPTER SIX

"So, you really went to an art museum? Jane, that's wonderful!"

"I guess." Jane's pen moved across the paper, adding a spray of flowers to the word "MEH" scrawled in near-perfect Vivaldi font.

"I mean it," Mrs. Baker continued. "Just follow your passion. It will guide you to happiness!" *That* was overkill. Like many parents, Jane's mom felt it was her job to be a cheering committee, telling Jane to be blissfully happy when she was really just neutral. In fact, she also did that when Jane was flat out miserable. But why? What was wrong with reality? As her mom continued to gush about how nice it was that Jane was getting back to her normal, cheery self—as if *that* was a thing—Jane added eyerolling faces to her doodle. How nice it must be for her mom to live in such a simple fantasyland.

Where did all this optimism come from? It certainly wasn't healthy, and telling Jane she could do anything she set her mind to was just setting her up to fail.

Which is why, though she loved her mom, Jane didn't really confide in her. Parents lied to their kids all the time. They said life was a dream, and happiness was attainable, and that when they grew up, they could be anything they wanted. *Lie.* You think you can become President of the United States if you really put your mind to it? No, you can't. One or two people can but everybody else can't. And the couple that can have a shitload of money, pedigree degrees from Harvard, and come from families of well-connected CEOs who scoff at people without summer homes in the Hamptons.

Nope, very few kids were going to grow up to be president. And really, who the hell would want that much responsibility anyway? People just wanted to make it through the work week so they could spend two days doing nothing. Not everyone wanted to live in a world of high achievement and charity galas.

Lightning strike! Jane was going to write a children's book. But not a rich, white person, hobby-job type of children's book. A real, tell it like it is, undo-the-lies-parents-tell children's book. It would help future generations to get a dose of reality at a young age.

She may have been a little bit buzzed, but Jane was pretty sure this idea was gold.

She got off the phone with her mom and got to work. Filling up her third glass of wine—or was it the fourth?—Jane started to think about all of the things parents say. First off, parents always tell their kids to work hard, and that hard work pays off. Well. Working hard was over rated. Sure, people should do enough that they have money to do fun things like drink and travel and pay for HBO-Go, but millionaire lawyer money is unnecessary.

Kids should be taught to work hard for a while, but not too hard because no matter what, the odds were against attaining their wildest dreams. In fact, wild dreams were bullshit. "Love what you do and you'll never work a day in your life" was a lie. A big, fat, stupid lie. She sketched furiously, drawing a woman with her head on a desk, next to a placard that read "I love my job."

What else? Oh, "you get what you give." That was *certainly* not true. If people got what they gave, she'd have been fired years ago. Alas, mediocrity had yielded many promotions. Jane scribbled a picture of an uneven scale with a question mark on one side and the words "it doesn't really matter" on the other.

The biggest bullshit to correct was that when you grow up you'll be happy, and that young adulthood would be "the best days of your life." Adults didn't have to be depressed and negative all the time, but you didn't turn eighteen and suddenly get super powers to create the life you want. This. Was. Bullshit. She drew a birthday cake with 18 candles and a middle finger.

Jane grinned. She was blowing her own mind. Her niece and nephew would be her first guinea pigs with her new life lessons. They would be so glad to have Aunt Jane's wisdom. She wished she'd known an adult like herself when she was a kid. For God's sake, her parents let her think she could grow up to be a fireman-princess. That's not even a thing! Certainly, her parents knew that in order to be a princess, one had to be born royal or marry a royal. Her bloodline was nowhere near blue enough and in the U.S. the nuptial back-up plan was extremely unlikely (well done, Markle).

And even if she had somehow snagged royalty for a husband, who the hell would allow a princess to fight fires? Nobody. Literally nobody. She sketched out a princess fighting fires, dress in flames, and royal guards holding their faces aghast. Oh man, she was going to turn the parenting world up-side-down. No more lies to kids!

This was good. It felt positive. Surprisingly, Jane was feeling fairly happy as of late. Why bring herself down by thinking of a missed life in which she became a super famous painter? That hadn't happened. But she did have a decent job, a cute apartment, and good friends. Sure, she wished she'd held on to art a bit harder. Dave as well. But these days they were both starting to come back to her, slowly but surely.

"In conclusion," she wrote, "current adult life consists mostly of complaining about where you've landed and reconsidering your life choices, knowing full well that different choices would have landed you in a similar position. I'm trying to help you avoid the pain and heartache that comes with this realization. If you can keep your goals realistic, you may come out on top. Don't reach for the stars—it's physically impossible to grab them. Reach for, like, 6-7 feet in the air!"

Perfect. She threw her pen down, exhausted from her hard work. She couldn't wait to test her material on Christine's children! She certainly deserved another drink after this masterpiece. She reached for the bottle, only to find it empty. Well shit. When had that happened? Oh well. She leaned back into her couch, curled up her feet and grabbed the remote. "A job well done," she told the Real Housewives.

But the Housewives didn't answer her. Who could she tell of her amazingness? She quickly grabbed her phone. But Elle just told her "sleep it off, drunkie," and Christine didn't answer. Oh! Dave! Mr. Always Online Dave would answer!

She messaged him via Facebook. *Dave! I did a thing so good!* Nice. Send.

A few seconds later her phone buzzed with an incoming text.

Janey. Do tell. The switch to text made her smile. Phones were more personal.

I did a book! For kids! To tell them their dreams can't come true!!!

HAHAHAHAAAA, Dave sent. Followed by, *That sounds amazing. What inspired this?*

Dave was getting it. This book would be huge!

My mom always used to tell me to just be happy but it's not that easy. And then I was thinking of all the lies parents tell their kids so I de-bunked some stuff. It's kind of a self-help book. Should be good!!! She followed that with five emojis: a trophy, a girl dancing, raising the roof, and two dogs for good measure.

You're gonna light the parenting world on fire. I'm proud of you. You deserve a drink!

OMG he was right! But shit, didn't he know her bottle was empty? *My bottle is empty.*

Aw, if I were home, I'd come bring you some more.

He wasn't home? Who was he out with? She felt a curl of unease flit through her drunken euphoria.

A date? she messaged, and waited with bated breath.

No Janey. Not a date. With Gracie.

Whew! *That's good. That you're with Gracie I mean. Not it's good that you don't have a date.* Wait, she didn't need to encourage him to date! *I mean, I'm not trying to tell you that you shouldn't date anyone. You're a grown-ass man, you know what you wanna do with your love life. Or not do. Either way, I'm cool.* Fuck. She sooo wasn't cool! Get it together, Jane!

She was about to try to back pedal that clusterfuck of texts when she saw three dots at the bottom of their thread and a new message came through.

You're adorable, he wrote. *Go get some sleep, my Janey. I'll talk to you again soon.* "My Janey"!?! Her grin practically split her face.

An accomplished Jane went to sleep, satisfied at the mark she'd made on the literary world and even more so after her conversation with Dave.

* * *

The next morning as Christine settled in at the office her frustration grew. Not only were things with Paul not ideal, but her client wouldn't budge for a seller asking only $2,000 more. At this rate he was going to lose the house over two grand. That's sofa money. Stupid men.

She got up to stretch her legs and get a cup of coffee in the hub down the hall.

"Hey you," she heard behind her as she sipped her freshly poured cup. She didn't have to turn around to know who the silky voice belonged to, but she did.

"Hey yourself," she said cocking her head slightly to the side. God, was she a high-schooler? She probably looked so stupid. She chastised herself until Frankie took an undeniable step closer.

"So, what are you doing after work today? I've got some more questions for you and would love to meet up again. Can I take you out for a drink?"

Christine paused.

"A purely professional meeting, of course," Frankie added, smiling that killer smile of his.

Nobody calls a meeting "purely professional" unless it isn't. It's kind of assumed that a work meeting is professional. But still, what if he did have more questions? She was one of the senior realtors on the team; she was really the best one to help him. And if a little harmless flirting was also involved so what? The kids were going to a friend's house after school so she didn't have to be home right away.

"Sure, I can do that. I've got to be home by six though."

"Ooh, husband keep a tight leash?" Frankie joked.

"No, nothing like that," Christine answered. She noticed how vague she had kept her response, and how she'd avoided mentioning her children. Frankie knew she had kids, but there was no need to remind him. She wanted to be fun and free, wanted him to see her as fun and free, if only for a minute.

"Great, I'll come by your desk around four-thirty then. We can cut out a little early."

"Perfect," Christine responded. She felt giddy, and a little guilty, but she was going. It wasn't a big deal, she reminded herself. They were just grabbing a drink. Paul did it with coworkers all the time.

At four-thirty sharp, Frankie knocked on her ajar office door.

"Ready to get out of here?" he asked as he leaned against the door frame.

God, he was good looking. Had guys looked that good when she was younger? Come to think of it, how old was he exactly? Christine was almost afraid to confirm his age. She knew it began with a two, which already made her feel like a predator. *Not that she was doing anything wrong!* Just drinks with a coworker.

"Ready," she responded.

She said goodbye to others as they left the building. Nobody gave Chris and Frankie any looks. Why would they? Who was she to think a twenty-something guy with muscles for days stretching his buttoned-down cabernet colored shirt until the seams were screaming would be into her?

They talked shop on the way to Cable's Bar and Grille around the corner. Frankie hugged the hostess, a gorgeous millennial blonde. Embarrassment heated Chris's cheeks. Of course he wasn't interested in her when he could go for a woman like the hostess.

As they sat down at the bar, Frankie turned and leaned toward her in a way that made her suddenly question everything. His knees brushed against hers, then pulled back but only slightly. Chris could feel his knee-heat across the small synapse of air that separated them.

"I'm so flattered you agreed to meet with me," Frankie began. *He* was flattered? "I really admire you. You're like a real-estate guru." Ok, this really was a work meeting. "You're so smart and cool." Wait, *was* it a work meeting? "And, I know I'm not supposed to say this, but I find you so sexy."

This was *not* a work meeting.

"Y...you do?" Christine sputtered back.

"Do you not know how sexy you are? I am ridiculously attracted to you. And I mean that with no disrespect. I know you're married and I'm not trying to take it there. I just hope you know you're beautiful. Your husband is one lucky guy." He smiled in such a sincere way it made Christine catch her breath. He meant all of this! "God, I've made you uncomfortable. I'm sorry. I swear I really do have work questions..."

Then something came over Christine that she didn't expect.

Panic set in as Frankie inched away from the sexy talk. She didn't want to talk about work. She wanted to talk about this. She put her arm on his, looked him dead in the eye, and said, "Fuck work."

Frankie flashed his dangerous smile. "Ok, fuck work," he agreed. "Tell me more about you."

"What do you want to know?" Chris asked earnestly, a shyness entering her voice.

"Everything," he replied, and her bashfulness dissipated immediately.

Conversation bounced between the two of them effortlessly. Chris talked about her parents and Jane and even her kids. Frankie talked about growing up in the Midwest, college, and the loneliness he'd felt when he first moved to L.A. The talk was meaningful and G-rated so Christine's guilt was at a minimum. She felt like they had a connection, but also that she'd done nothing to feel ashamed about. No overt flirting, no long staring, no asking him if she could sample his lips while feeling all those gorgeous muscles...Nope, no shame here.

With no lulls in conversation, finally Frankie excused himself to use the restroom. Chris glanced at her watch. Oh fuck, it was almost six! Time had flown and she had to go. She didn't want this early evening to end but it had to. Jane was coming over later (some text last night about a kids' book she'd written? Who knew, she seemed drunk) and Paul wouldn't be home until well after eight. The kids couldn't feed themselves.

When Frankie came back, she broke the news. "I didn't realize how late it was. I actually have to get going."

"Oh, sure. No problem." Frankie went to pay the check, but Christine had already done so when he was in the bathroom.

"You didn't have to get this, really. I invited you out," he said as he looked at her intensely.

"It was my pleasure." She had never meant that so much.

They walked out and didn't discuss meeting up again. But Christine had a good feeling he'd ask her out again soon. After all, they'd already been texting.

She shook her head. God, what was she doing? She was a married woman! But this was all innocent. So, she'd had some drinks and made a new friend. Everyone wanted their friends to text them. And if he asked her for drinks again, she could do that. Just drinks with a coworker. Maybe a friend.

Definitely not a lover.

On her drive home, Chris's phone buzzed, making her heart jump. Was it him already? She glanced at her phone at a stoplight. Jane. She'd be late.

Instead of replying right away like she usually did, she selected an old Cyndi Lauper song from her phone and blared it over her Bluetooth, singing like an American Idol the entire way home.

Once in the door, Chris whisked into action, changing into more comfortable clothes and getting dinner for the kids. She found herself thinking back on her evening with Frankie with pleasure, and realized she was smiling like an idiot. Before Jane arrived, Chris knew she'd have to divert her or Jane would suspect something was up. So when her sister walked through the door, Chris blurted out, "I seriously think Paul is cheating on me." No better way to deflect than to air the old grievance, right?

"I know you do, but you're wrong. He loves you."

"He's been working early and late almost every day lately."

"Early? Who has morning affairs?" Jane asked earnestly. Chris gave her side-eye and Jane realized more of her was required. "Why don't you just ask him about it?"

"I have. He gets defensive."

"You're way more likely to have an affair than he is," Jane said nonchalantly. Chris hit her little sister with a pillow. She tried to push down a ping in her stomach at the thought of how Frankie looked a few hours ago in the muted bar light.

"You're right. I should talk to him again."

It was now Jane's turn to provide the side-eye, as Christine's voice had an audible ring of bullshit to it.

Chris was not a bullshitter.

"Wait a sec. Is this one of those moments from the movies where one person accuses another of cheating, because they themselves are cheating? Chris, do you *want* him to be having an affair? Are *you* having an affair?"

Christine turned toward her sister with a look of confusion. Though she was most certainly not cheating on her husband, something in Jane's words did cut through. She wasn't sure she was ready yet to admit it out loud, but maybe she had been secretly hoping Paul was cheating on her. That way, she'd be guilt free to do whatever she wanted with Frankie.

Not that she was going to do anything!

"No. I'm not cheating on Paul," she said in her serious-big-sister-is-serious voice, designed to shut Jane down immediately. Jane got the hint, and changed topics, thank God.

Out of her backpack, she pulled out a bunch of pages stapled messily together. Across the front, written in fairytale scrolls, it read "Mommy and Daddy are Liars." Oh God, what was this?

"Taa-daa!" Jane exclaimed as she handed it to Christine. "It's a children's book and I want Lucy and Cameron to read it!"

Taking in the title, Christine did not hold back. "Jane, I'm obviously never showing this to my children."

"Just read it!" Jane huffed. Chris reluctantly took the book. Her little sister was so pushy.

Christine eyed her skeptically, poured them each a glass of white wine, and sat down at the dining room table to peruse the book. It was printed on regular computer paper but Jane had taped in some sketches.I It was nice to see Jane creating again, and she'd obviously put work into her sketches. They were quite good; it was the accompanying words that had her cringing on the inside. Chris took a moment to reflect on how long it had been since she'd seen her sister's art.

"So?" Jane asked impatiently. "What do you think?" Her eyes gleamed with excitement.

Chris didn't want to take that away, but …"I…I…can't believe you're drawing again," she replied, completely glossing over the rest of the book. "Jane, this is amazing."

"Really? Thanks! I wasn't sure if the text read too negative."

"Oh honey, not the text. The text is crazy." Yeah, sometimes the truth hurt. "But the art, Jane. The art is amazing. I'd forgotten how good you are."

"Um, thanks," Jane replied lamely. It clearly wasn't the answer she wanted.

Christine went on. "See, I don't have a passion like yours. I mean, I care about a lot of things, but you *are* art. I've always known that. You giving it up kept me awake at night. I wanted to make you change your mind. But I just knew you were so stubborn that there was nothing I could do to get you back to it."

Jane avoided making eye contact. Probably because she was close to tears, Chris realized. Her sister had always been a softie at heart.

Eventually, after helping Chris clean up the remains of dinner and load the dishes, Jane got ready to leave. As Chris hugged her goodbye, she couldn't resist one more big-sister-knows-best moment.

"Hey Jane? The reason we tell children to reach for the stars is because people need goals to work toward. Because you're right. You don't always get what you want. Some people want to be NFL players so they play college football. And they may not end up going pro, but they do get a college degree. What would've happened if they never had a goal?"

She could tell Jane took a moment to consider this. "I don't know, Chris. Mom and Dad always encouraged me in art and I thought that fucked me up. But maybe you have a point," she mused. "Where would I be now if my office job was the original goal? A gas station?"

"Exactly," Chris piped in. "And Jane. I know you don't want to hear this but you don't know how far you would've gotten if you'd stuck with art."

"I guess you're right." Jane paused. "But seriously though... shouldn't parents tone it down a liiiittle?"

Chris laughed. There was her sister's wry humor. "Yeah, maybe we should."

* * *

Elle was supposed to meet her next app date at eight in the magazine section at a bookstore to grab coffee and take a walk through the adjacent outdoor mall. From his photos, she wasn't entirely certain what he would look like. He looked racially ambiguous, kind of like Maya Rudolph. She also couldn't tell what his body type was; in some photos he looked a bit heavy; in others he was rail thin. Granted, she didn't care much what his physique was like. But she was not at all confident she'd recognize him if he were standing right in front of her.

At 8:10 she texted him to make sure she didn't miss him. *Turns out there's a magazine dedicated to monster trucks and the men who drive them. #TheMoreYouKnow.* Now he'd at least know she was here.

A few seconds later, a ridiculously hot human being approached her. "Are you Elle?"

"Yeah, um, hi," she managed. He was sooo much more attractive than his photos had indicated! This guy was a straight-up Jesse Williams type. He had light-dark skin, piercing blue eyes, and a few freckles perfectly sprinkled across his face. Seriously, the man was drool-worthy. She surreptitiously wiped her lip (just in case!).

They walked toward the coffee shop section of the store and her date, whose name was Tom, started the conversation.

"So, what do you do?" he asked.

Flustered by his good looks, she took a moment. What did she do again? Oh yeah, kids!

"I'm a social worker. I work with teens--" she began.

"My ex is a social worker," Tom interrupted harshly. Bringing up the ex on a first date, hmm. Though a faux-pas, it definitely happened on the regular. At least, that's what the kids at the center would say. As someone who didn't really date, Elle didn't know all the rules. But bringing up the ex immediately seemed not a great sign.

So social work was obviously not a good topic. What now? When in doubt, ask about him. People always liked to talk about themselves. "What about you? What do you do?"

Tom was a chef and had recently come from Seattle for reasons he wouldn't say, though Elle had a sneaking suspicion the ex had something to do with it. Thank God he was so hot, or she might have to care.

As they waited in line for the coffee, Elle and Tom spoke of generalities: life in Los Angeles, their tastes in music, how awesome his ex was. You know, general, every day, first date stuff.

Meandering through the outdoor mall they noticed a crowd had formed at one end. Evidently, it was free movie night at the mall. Because God is real, the movie was a 90s action flick. Elle was in heaven. She knew the film well, and quickly explained the entire back story to Tom who seemed amused that this was so deep in her wheelhouse.

Elle felt confident that he was kind of digging her, but was she digging him? They walked a bit more and Tom piped up.

"Can I say something?" he started.

Elle immediately tensed; nothing good ever came after that question. "Yeah. Of course."

"I know I've brought up my ex a few times. I know that's not cool. I'm over her, I swear."

"Ok..."

"I'm new to L.A. and it can be lonely. She's on my mind because she's my most recent, but I'm ready to move on. I just wanted you to know that."

Hmm. Well played, Jesse "Tom" Williams. Maybe it wasn't a red flag after all; Elle still thought about Lilly on occasion. Granted, she hadn't brought her up multiple times tonight. But if she were in a new city all alone, who knew? Tom had officially earned himself another date. And *damn* was he hot.

"No problem. I get it. I had fun tonight," she added.

Elle took her time meandering back to her car. The fresh air felt good, and the people watching was great. Tonight hadn't been an A+ but Tom had potential.

By the time she got to her car, he had texted to ask when he could see her next. Elle immediately forwarded the message to Jane with a few exclamation points to let her know she had scored a second date. Jane replied with a thumbs-up emoji, followed by a message simply stating "Meeting Dave tomorrow" and a nervous smile emoji.

CHAPTER SEVEN

Jane sat in a booth at Rae's Diner, fidgeting as though her life depended on it. She looked around the turquoise and wood-laden restaurant which hadn't changed a bit since she'd last been there years before. A faint, permanent smell of scrambled eggs and coffee sat in the air as headshots of stars from the 80s and 90s speckled the walls. The minutes passed at an ungodly slow rate, Jane noticed, as she checked her phone nearly constantly.

She thought about what Chris had said yesterday as she was leaving the house. Ugh, now that she was (currently) sober, she could see how her negativity oozed from that children's book. Of course Chris wouldn't want to give it to Cameron and Lucy. What had she been thinking? She hadn't, Jane could now acknowledge in the sober light of day. She'd just been pouring out her own disappointment with life.

But Chris, in her usual motherly way, turned it around. It was true, Jane had been bitter for years. It was also true that she was finally pulling her head out of her ass and trying at life again. She was trying to find Ridgeley, trying to do some art again, and here she was, about to try with Dave.

If he'd ever show up.

She reached over to check her phone again and there he was. The air left the room as the door swung open and Dave walked through, a glowing ball of sunshine. He carried a huge grin and the heat within him still burned bright, hot enough to scorch her even this far away.

Jane took off her jacket. Her stomach was somewhere on the floor, and there was no way she'd be able to eat with all of these raw nerves hanging out. Thank God she'd predicted this and wolfed down a bagel right before she left her house. Dave didn't have to guess where she'd be sitting; she was in the booth they used to live in. It practically had their 18-year-old bodies imprinted in the seats. Jane couldn't believe how long it had been since she'd been in here and, more importantly, in the presence of her friend.

As he approached, a bit of a calm settled over Jane, just enough to put light protective caps on her nerve endings. She knew this man. He was no stranger. This was her Dave. (Ridgeley's Dave? No, fuck that. HER Dave.) As he neared the table, Jane felt herself standing up. She stepped out of the booth and looked up at his warm, heated face.

"Well, holy shit," Dave said as they enveloped each other in the world's most overdue hug. Jane wasn't much of a long embrace type of hugger. But she wasn't letting go of her friend just yet. They squeezed each other's backs, ruffed each others' hair and finally sat down.

"Yeah, holy shit indeed," Jane finally responded. The waitress (a total Nancy) came over and without thinking Dave ordered their old usual, a black decaf coffee for him and a hot water with lemon and extra honey for Jane. She hadn't drunk that in years, but man did it sound good. And he'd remembered her old favorite!

"Hey Janey. What'd you name the waitress in your head?"

Holy, shit, he remembered that! "Nancy," she replied, not missing a beat.

"I love that you still do that," Dave said followed by a moment of silence between the two friends.

"Where do we even start?" Jane asked helplessly. And, like the lifeline he had always been, Dave tossed her a buoy in the form of pulling out his phone and talking her through his Facebook pictures. His hand brushed hers as he turned to show her his phone. Sparks ignited in her stomach. Oh God, what did that mean? Was she still into Dave after all these years, or was it simply her inner 18-year-old acting up? She'd think about it later. Time to focus on Dave.

Dave was happy. He had close friends, lived near his sister, had a decent job as a contractor, and spent many weekends playing beach volleyball. He showed her a vacation he took with his best friend Alex, the time he was the best man at Gracie's wedding, and an action shot of him diving into the sand gracelessly as the volley-ball bounced feet in front of his outreaching hands. He had a few pictures of sunsets but they no longer made him cry (she asked). He had some cool shots of random city scenes but he no longer went on adventure walks (she asked). He had very few shots of his face close up but he was still hot as hell (she didn't have to ask).

When it came Jane's turn to play the "what's up with me game," she didn't know where to start. She had been careful to avoid deep personal stuff over messaging, but now it was time to fill Dave in. Taking a page out of Dave's book, she pulled out her phone. Her profile picture was her looking awkwardly awful in a candid shot Elle had taken of her throwing something at the T.V. She filled him in on who Elle was, which brought a smile to her face. Next, a shot of Christine who he naturally remembered. Then, she opened up her folder of photos and began to walk Dave through them. She was surprised to see that her life in pictures didn't seem all that bad. In fact, she had a lot of happy times. Most involved Elle and her at a bar or on her couch, but nonetheless they were happy. A photo of Christine's kids popped up and Jane introduced them to Dave.

When she'd scrolled through about twenty pictures, and told the sarcastic or darkly funny stories that accompanied most of them, she stopped. She'd apologized over text but that wasn't enough. "Dave. I'm so fucking sorry. We've missed each other's lives and it's literally all my fault. I'm an asshole."

Dave looked at her for a beat—the longest pause of her life. "Hey asshole. I forgive you."

And that was that.

After they finished their drinks and shared the diner's famous triple-layer chocolate cake, conversation turned to the Ridgeley hunt.

"I just hope this art teacher recognizes her name. I can't even show her what she looks like."

Dave looked at Jane as though she was a kindergartener. "Jane. C'mon."

"What?"

"Why don't you draw her?"

"Oh my God. Why the fuck didn't I think of that?"

He polished off the dregs of his second cup of coffee. She tried not to notice the strong lines of his throat. Was he tightening his jaw on purpose? "Well, you know, sometimes it's easy to miss things that are right in front of you."

Jane shifted awkwardly, not knowing how deeply to look into the comment.

She immediately pulled a pen out of her purse, grabbed a napkin, and began to sketch. Having Dave there proved hugely helpful; it turned out her mind's eye was missing some details on what Ridgeley looked like. "She had a dimple on one cheek, remember? It popped out when she smiled," Dave said nostalgically.

Jane almost puked and punched him at the same time. He was testing her control with comments like these. "Ok, I get it, she's amazing. Be objective," she scolded Dave.

"And her nose, it was delicate and curled up slightly at the end."

Really, really testing her. Was that a smirk on his face?

"And her eyes were a little more dreamy than that, full of sparkles."

Jane gritted her teeth, "Dave, I swear to God—"

Then he burst out laughing. "Oh, Janey, I'm just teasing. You always were cute when you got annoyed. I just wanted to see if that still held true."

Jane grumbled, but she couldn't keep her lips from quirking in a smile.

By the end of the back and forth, they both agreed that the sketch bore a pretty decent resemblance to the memory they had of Ridgeley from fifteen years before. Jane put the picture in her purse for safe keeping. "That was fun," Dave said. And though she hadn't loved hearing Dave describe the subject matter, Jane reluctantly agreed.

But of course, hanging out with Dave was always fun.

Due to their teamwork, she thought her drawing ended up pretty damn accurate. And now she had a tool in her belt to show Angela Ashbury, and hopefully get closer to finding Ridgeley and the painting.

* * *

Elle was prepping for her next date with Tom. He'd suggested bowling, which made her happy. It was more interesting than meeting at a bar—not that there was anything wrong with that!—and truth be told, she was kind of a great bowler.

Walking into the alley, she spotted Tom in the arcade section and practically lost her breath. What was it about this dude? He was so gorgeous Elle couldn't think straight. God, their kids would be beautiful!

At the lanes, Tom suggested they choose fake names for the scoreboard.

"What about Jesse Williams for you?" she offered, recalling her first impression of him.

"Like the actor? Nah, I mean something like this." He typed in *Tom the Tiger*. It wasn't hilarious but it wasn't horribly embarrassing so she considered it a win and went with *Elle-ectric* for herself.

Elle kicked Tom's ass bowling (and he was a gracious loser,

so points in his favor), and they moved across the street to an ice cream parlor. They chatted about the flavors and a bit about bowling. He mentioned his ex briefly but caught himself and changed the subject! Finishing dessert, they decided to prolong the date by taking a walk. But as they meandered through the neighborhood a bit, Elle realized she was running out of things to say. Gah. Why was dating so awkward?

After a seemingly endless, but likely only 30-second bout of silence, Tom jumped in. "It's nice, isn't it, when you get to that point with someone where you don't have to talk because it's just comfortable." He paused. "That's what I like about being in a relationship." He squeezed her hand.

Elle appreciated the gesture, although the type of comfort he was referring to was found after years of solid foundation had been built with a person, not on date two. Also, they were categorically *not* in a relationship. Nonetheless, he had broken the silence, which was more than she could say for herself. To thank him for doing so, and, let's face it, because he was so sexy, Elle leaned in and kissed him. They embraced, softly cradling each other's faces, their lips moving a bit more feverishly. She heard Tom emit the slightest moan under his breath. *Oh, yeah.* The move was effective. Elle was definitely thinking about more than kissing. She pushed forward and kissed him harder, feeling butterflies flutter through her stomach and lower.

"I could really see myself with you," Tom whispered in her ear. "We could take walks like this every night. Just the two of us together. Well, maybe someday with a baby stroller." He paused as Elle stared at him blankly. "Oh God, that's too much for a second date. Sorry. Sometimes by daydreams run away with me."

Elle smiled. He was probably just nervous. Sure that was way too much for a second date, but

she had almost doubled down on Ireland before even meeting him. And she liked that Tom was relationship minded.

"It's cool," said.

With that, Tom returned to exploring her mouth with his and all bets were off. Elle could feel the buzz of excitement in her lower belly. Her hands ran over Tom's delightful muscles in anticipation of a fun-filled night. But shit! She had promised Jane no sex until at least three dates in. *Why had she done that?* Squeezing his shoulder gently, she pulled back from his glorious face. "I should go," she said painstakingly.

Tom, taking her statement at face value, walked her back to her car. He didn't try to come home with her or say anything cheesy, which she appreciated. He simply asked when he could see her again.

On the way home, Elle oscillated between smiles and slight grimaces. Tom really was sweet. But that shit about a baby stroller was pretty weird. They barely knew each other. In a snap decision, she pulled over and parked alongside the well-lit street and hopped out of the car. Walking always cleared her head.

Tom hadn't mentioned his ex (as much) on this date, which was a plus. The guy was clearly down for something serious, which also boded well. And he was obviously into her. He even said he could see himself with her. But he didn't know her; they'd only been out twice. Maybe she just needed to let her guard down. Afterall, she wanted a relationship too. What was wrong with a guy who wanted the same?

She was sick of hook-ups and this guy was clearly not just aiming for sex! He was fun, and nice and *goddamn* was he hot. Head cleared, she decided she'd give Tom another shot. Hopping back in her car, she checked her phone to see a message from Tom. *I can't wait to see you again, baby.*

* * *

Chris put away the boxes of Crayons and told Cameron and Lucy it was time to get ready for bed. Paul, obviously at "work." Christine and the kids had spent the evening coloring. It was Lucy's idea. She'd asked to see Aunt Jane, but Chris wanted some quality time with her kids. The next best thing to having Jane there was doing the thing Jane loved most: art. The kids' imaginations took over their hands as the crayons blazed across the paper.

"Mommy, look what I drew!" an emphatic Lucy shouted.

Knowing better than to mislabel the drawing, a skilled Chris responded, "Wow, Lucy, it's *beautiful.*"

"Guess what it is?" Lucy baited.

"It's too pretty I can't. You made it. You tell *me* about it."

"It's a pink dragon named Dandy and she has butterfly wings."

"I love her. But not as much as I love the two of you!" she added, attacking her kids with kisses.

As Cameron always drew space monsters, she didn't have to try hard to identify his work.

Cleaning up, she sent her kids upstairs to get ready for bed. Lucy ran toward her pajamas, but Cameron hung back. His little face looked so solemn.

"What's up honey?" Chris asked, bending down to Cameron's level. This wasn't about wanting to stay up.

He started to say "Nothing," but then blurted out, "Dad's been gone a lot. But you haven't." And he threw himself into her arms with abandon.

The recognition and sweet toddler hugs from her son sent jolts of happiness through her body. Her home life had felt like such a fail lately; she needed that.

After tucking in her tuckered-out kids, Chris headed down to the couch for some wine and relaxation. Her phone buzzed and electricity jolted through her when she saw who had texted.

Hi, Frankie wrote.

She couldn't. Not after that comment from Cameron. Plus, Paul should actually be home soon.

Like clockwork, her phone buzzed again.

Running later than I thought, sorry. Tell the kids goodnight for me, Paul sent.

Chris wanted to rage at him. At least he could call and tell them himself. But it's hard to talk to your kids with some other woman's tongue down your throat. Fuck it. At this point, Chris didn't owe Paul a thing. Ignoring her husband, she messaged Frankie back.

Hi. Simple enough, and inoffensive.

You looked amazing today :) he sent.

You didn't look so bad yourself. Ok, that was a bit over the line, but her husband was out sleeping with someone else, so what harm would flirting do?

What are you doing right now? Frankie asked.

Downing her wine, inspiration hit her. She stood up, refilled her glass, and situated herself perfectly on the couch. Smiling seductively, Chris flipped the camera function on her phone and took her first selfie. *Oh God, that was awful.* How did younger people do this? Taking a few minutes to mess with angles and lighting, she finally snapped a sendable selfie. With her arm extended above her, the camera peered down at her upturned face and caught her cleavage. *Perfect!*

This, she captioned the pic. *What are you doing?*

Frankie took a moment to respond, and then *bam!* A picture of him shirtless, muscles flexed and a wry smile on his face.

Chris stared at her phone, attempting not to drool. *I like it.* she bit her lip as she hit send.

Christine, I like your picture very much. Too much.

Oh my God, what was she doing? Ok, this was flirtatious but it's not like they were sending nudes. And it's not like she was having an actual affair, which is more than she could say about Paul! Yes! She could flirt as much as she wanted, as long as it didn't get physical!

Tell me how much... she sent back.

Let's just say it had a... physical effect.

Chris squealed. She couldn't do this! But she was loving it. But she was a married woman! Even if Paul was stepping out, this had gone far enough. She had to take a step back.

Good to know;) Alright, I'm off to bed. Nite.

It wasn't a full pumping of the breaks but it was good enough for tonight.

CHAPTER EIGHT

All day Jane had faked her way through work, mentally prepping herself to take the next step toward finding Ridgeley. Finally, it was time. She jumped in her car and made her way toward Angela Ashbury's class. This was good. It could be the link that brought her to the missing painting. But she had to leave before the class started. Sure, she'd been drawing a bit lately but the idea of an actual lesson made bile rise in her stomach. She'd escape before it came to that. Pumping Fleetwood Mac, she pulled into the parking lot, checking her expectations.

It'd be great to find Ridgeley herself here, but Jane knew that was unlikely. Ridgeley would have to be still living in Los Angeles, and also free of obligations, and also taking this specific art class on the exact night that Jane chose to pop in. And honestly, the Universe never aligned that perfectly.

Ugh, "the Universe"? She figuratively punched herself in the face in Elle's honor.

Jane stepped into the stucco-covered, one-story building and panned the room. Immediately recognizing it as Ridgeley-free, she searched the room for someone in charge and came up blank. She saw a Skye, a River and an Ashlynn but no Angela. As she looked for a seat, rustling at the door grabbed her attention. A tall brunette with lightly salted brown hair pulled into a loose bun walked into the room. She looked like a divorcée from a 1960s movie. All she needed was a silk robe and a cigarette holder. That was definitely Angela. The feminine figure sauntered into the room with an authoritative air, moved to the front, and waited until she had everyone's attention. "Good evening everyone, and nice to see so many familiar faces. Tonight, we're going back to basics. Using charcoal, we'll be focusing on essence and value. Focus on the foreground and show me clean gradations."

Damn. It was too late to talk to Angela now. Looking around the room, she considered her options. She could leave and wait outside, hoping to catch Angela on the way out. Or… she could stay and take the class, upping her odds of getting an in with the teacher during the lesson. Even if Jane couldn't drill her while Angela gave notes on charcoal technique, it was much more likely she'd talk to a student after class than a perfect stranger.

Swallowing her nerves, Jane relented. She would take her first art class since sophomore year of college.

She took her place in front of an easel, charcoal pieces awaiting

106

her in the rails. Jane took in the metal sculpture at the front of the room. She reached for the charcoal.

And it all came back.

Like no time had been lost, her hand moved swift and sure. Jane got on her proverbial bicycle and began to outline the form, curving the charcoal ever so slightly at the first bend, careful not to press into the paper overmuch to avoid creating a chalky texture. She tilted her head as she danced the charcoal across the page.

Ugh. *Danced the charcoal across the page.* Who was she, an 18-year-old art student who wore black all the time and went to indy movies? Jesus. Back to the easel.

It was twenty minutes into the class before she realized that Angela had passed her three times without a word. Lost in her own work, Jane decided she'd better save the drilling until after class. She heard Angela whisper as she walked by another student. Several head nods were awarded to others, and as Angela passed Jane for the fourth time, she heard a quiet but notable, "Nice" as she viewed Jane's work.

Satisfaction flooded over Jane like the first sip of red wine after a long day. So familiar, yet so foreign. It was like an outfit she'd forgotten in the back of her closet that still fit perfectly. She reveled in the feeling of the coal between her fingers, the powdery black falling onto the floor like a warm, dark flurry. As she eyed the sculpture she nearly forgot to look at her own page. She knew the movements of her hands so well that her hand-eye coordination became a direct line.

God, she'd missed this.

Her charcoal piece broke, bringing her out of her trance just in time for a moment of doubt to creep in. Full of self-criticism, she looked around the room, expecting to feel the weight of failure. Surely the others were more talented than her. But no. She peeked at the easels near her. What she saw wasn't bad, not bad at all, but as she turned to finally take in her own lines her breath caught.

Hers was better.

The essence popped. The gradations were smooth.

But it wasn't even about comparing her work to anyone else's, not really. It was about her own sense of worth. Her picture was good, beautiful, even. She had captured an essence about the metal piece that the piece itself was fighting to hide, a certain whimsy that jumped off of her page.

With extra wind in her sails, she easily fell back into the zone and worked on her drawing until the class wound down. She was in a cloud as Angela thanked everyone for attending and collected payment. "Nice work today," Angela said as Jane handed her the class fee. "I haven't seen you before. Did you enjoy the class?"

It was as though Jane had swallowed a full dose of DayQuil. Half of her head was in a balloon. "Yeah," Jane fumbled.

"You've got some talent. But I can also tell you've had some training. Art Sherman's studio? Maybe Cassie Vance's?"

"No. I took a short break from art. Like a fifteen year…Today was my first time in a studio in a long time. It was thrilling. I…I don't know, thank you. Just, like, thanks." Smooth.

Jane turned to exit, then popped out of her daze and back into reality. Ridgeley! She had almost forgotten to ask. "Angela, can I ask you something?"

"Sure," the teacher responded openly.

"I saw online that you've worked with a lot of greats. Stephanie Serfshire. Tiana Ferrawhey."

"Yes, I've been teaching a long time so I've had run-ins with some pretty successful artists. Tiana used to come here when she was in her early 20s. Steel shell of an exterior, but the work poured out like liquid mercury."

"Wow that's … really cool."

As Angela started to talk about her more famous students of the past few years, Jane looked for a moment to jump in. "I'm wondering if you've ever had a student who went by the name of Ridgeley."

"Doesn't sound familiar. But then again, sometimes the students run together over time. Last name?"

"She only went by Ridgeley when I knew her."

"What is she, Cher?"

Jane snort-giggled. Seems Angela also didn't get Ridgeley's one-namedness. Jane approved.

She decided to go for broke. Her napkin sketch of Ridgeley was good, but was it good enough to spark actual recognition? There was one way to find out.

Jane reached into her purse and pulled out her napkin art. "Here, I drew a sketch of her." She passed over the sketch of Ridgeley and held her breath.

"Hmm. I can't be sure, but she does look familiar. That's a good sketch." Jane couldn't help but pocket the compliment to chew on later. "If she's who I think she is, I don't think I ever knew her name. She would drop in sometimes, but I haven't seen her since probably the late 90s." That sounded about right. "She signed her paintings funny," Angela added.

Holy shit! "With a picture of a cat?" she asked Angela.

"Yes, that's right."

Jane felt her excitement grow. "I'm trying to find her. Can you think of anything at all, any detail that might help me locate her?"

Angela took the question seriously. Jane watched her brow furrow in thought, and finally Angela struck gold. "It's not much, but we would sometimes talk about it when Fine Art added to their inventory. She shopped there too. It's a really great, small art supply store in Burbank."

A clue! Jane now officially knew where Ridgeley had purchased art supplies. She would have guessed various stores closer to campus, so this was good information. Of course, stores often had a high turn-over rate with employees, but hopefully someone there would recognize Jane's napkin art.

"Sorry I couldn't be of more help."

"No, you've been wonderful. Truly. And I really enjoyed the class," Jane said as she carefully carried out her first charcoal drawing in fifteen years.

Walking to her car, she barely noticed she was humming Joan Baez's "Diamonds and Rust." A familiar, if tiny, spark was beginning to awaken in her belly.

* * *

Elle met Tom at his place for dinner. The man had promised her a good, homecooked meal. Despite being more of a whiskey gal, Elle brought some wine to go with his Italian. A few minutes into the risotto, Tom mentioned his ex. "She's still in Seattle," he offered, apropos of nothing. "She's been calling me a lot lately. She thinks I owe her money."

That didn't bode well for the *is financially stable* part of her list.

"We were together for eight years. And we argued. She was

too messy for me, I didn't pay enough of the bills for her... But you know how it is. It's still better to be in an imperfect relationship than to be alone."

Wait, what?

"Nah, but we had our moments." He stared into the middle distance, smiling.

Elle opted to say nothing. What could she say to something like that? And was he really going to spend their date thinking about another woman? Why did he *always* bring her up? It was annoying, but she couldn't leave yet; she was hungry, after all. Plus, maybe he'd turn this around. He and his ex had broken up fairly recently. Everyone needed recovery time.

Tom looked at her sincerely. "I've been meaning to tell you," he began, "you're aging really well for a white person."

Elle choked on her pasta, then fell into a coughing and laughing fit. What the fuck? Who *says* that to a person? "Thanks," she finally mustered. "That's kind of you to say."

Tom beamed.

Elle shifted the conversation by asking about why his pictures on Buzz were so different from each other. Tom confided he'd recently lost some weight and had taken up working out. "You know, so my ex wouldn't move on right away. She told me during the breakup my pudge wasn't a turn on. I knew this would really piss her off, me getting fit."

Hmm. Homeboy was clearly not over the ex, so there was no place for Elle in his life. Welp, that was it then. Elle was going to update the list as soon as she got home: *over the ex.*

It was a shame, Elle mused, since Tom was an otherwise sweet guy, Jesse Williams looks notwithstanding. But she couldn't be with him if she was going to have to hear about this wonderful, infuriating ex all the time. Needing some time to process, Elle cut the night short, citing an early start for work. She wasn't ready for the "this isn't going to work" conversation.

The next day, scrolling through social media, Elle noticed Tom had liked several pictures of hers on Facebook from two and three years ago. He also messaged her asking if he could take her out for her birthday, which was months away. Then he started setting up the next date, but when she asked (just to see his response) what he had planned, his answer was, *What do you want to do, baby?*

This guy did not know how to date.

It was clear to Elle that Tom wanted to be in a relationship more than he wanted to be with *her*. For him, any woman would do. *Especially* his ex. He didn't know how to be alone, and she felt sorry for him. But that was not her problem.

She kicked him to the curb ever so gently, with a message stating that she felt they didn't have that connection and she didn't want to hang out any more. It felt kind of shitty to send, but it was better than ghosting.

Tom responded that he understood and wished her well. Elle patted herself on the back for ending the almost-relationship in a mature, grown-up way.

Too bad that wasn't the end of it.

Over the next few days, Tom messaged multiple times a day asking if they could hang out. *Just as friends, of course*, he'd written. He told her he missed her and that he wanted to go bowling again. Or to see a movie. Or to have dinner. Or how about they go to San Diego for the weekend?

The first day she had politely, but firmly, told him she'd rather make a clean break than attempt to be friends. The second day, he sent her a smiley face emoji with the message, *Miss your face! STOP*, she'd replied, as if unsubscribing to spam.

Completely ignoring her explicit request, on the third day he sent a gif of flowers being delivered with the words "Sending you love" scrawled across the bottom. Elle figured he was probably more desperate than dangerous but she was no fool and she wasn't fucking around.

Days four, five, and six were progressively more and more frustrating as Tom continued to bombard her phone and social media with emojis, gifs, texts, and song lyrics that "remind me of us". Finally, Elle pulled out the big guns. *I've tried to be clear. Ever heard the phrase no means no? Lose my fucking number or I'm calling the fucking police.*

Ew. She wasn't actually scared, seeing as the guy didn't know where she lived or worked, and she kept all of her private info off of social media (which she'd finally blocked him on). But the clinginess of this one! She felt slimed by his desperation. No wonder his ex had left him! She poured herself a whiskey and jumped in the bath to wash off the filth.

* * *

"Come in," Chris shouted toward the door. Clearly it was Elle, as Jane would've just walked right in.

"Yo. Brought some whiskey and chips!" Elle offered, sliding out of her leather jacket and tossing it over the back of the couch.

Chris took Elle's offerings and put them on the kitchen table as the front door popped open again.

"Party's here!" Jane announced.

This meet-up was long overdue. Sure, Jane saw Elle and Chris frequently, but the three women hadn't hung out together since the pact to take control over their own lives. They had vowed to change that and this was the first step.

Paul was (surprise) working late and the kids asleep. Thank God they were heavy sleepers, after Jane's entrance. The friends exchanged some small talk as the snacks were set up and the drinks were poured. Then it was time to dive a little deeper.

"So ladies, tell me everything I don't know," Chris opened.

Elle started. She filled Chris in on the Tom saga (Jane already mostly up-to-date).

"That's terrifying," Chris reacted.

"No, for real. He's stopped since then. And he doesn't know how to find me. Honestly, none of it was even about me. He's probably moved on to his next 'relationship.'"

"Some people just don't know how to be alone," Jane offered.

"Yeah, I see it at the center all the time, but I like to think people grow out of their unhealthy patterns before they're in their 40s. I guess the joke's on me!" Elle concluded.

"So Tom was a clingy nutcase, but a lot of people *have* grown out of their bullshit. Don't use this as an excuse to give up," Jane said. "Like Dave! He used to do a ton of stupid shit that he doesn't do any more. Like, he used to write poetry about his exes. I mean, it's not scary but it's lame as fuck and now he, like, does construction!"

Chris offered side-eye to the barely arguable comparison. "So, what's up with you and Dave anyway?" she segued.

"Nothing. I mean, we've been talking. I went to that art class and we chatted about it. And we've met up a couple times. But it's not like that. It's just nice having my friend back."

"Riiiight," Chris said.

"Yep. Totally believe you." Elle's voice dripping with sarcasm.

"Shut up." Jane paused. "Ok fine. Of course I'm into him. But how's that possible so soon? I haven't seen him in like fifteen years. Feelings that last that long have to be a fantasy. And obviously I know he's not 'the one' because 'the one' isn't a thing."

"Whoever said anything about 'the one'?" Elle asked.

"Yeah, you can be into him and still not believe in fairytales. I used to think Paul was 'the one'. That's just not how it works."

Elle piped up. "How *are* things with Paul?"

Chris shuffled uncomfortably. How *were* things with Paul? "I don't know. I mean, they're fine. Better."

"Hmm...I call bullshit," Jane said, peering intently at Chris. "Your face suggests you're lying."

"I don't know. I still think he's cheating. Look at right now! It's 8pm and he's not home. That's every day lately."

"Have you talked to him yet?" asked Jane for the hundredth time.

"There's no time to." And in that moment Chris's phone buzzed.

"Speak of the devil?" Elle asked.

Looking down at her phone Chris's heart jumped. Keeping her face as smooth as possible, she glanced at the text from Frankie and returned to her conversation.

"Yep. Paul's just checking in." Would her sister and Elle believe her? She was a terrible liar. Noting a look of doubt on Jane's face, she jumped back in to cause distraction.

"Did I mention that I've lost weight recently? I've been going to the gym and it's working. So that's going well."

"Good for you," Elle added, as Jane clinked her glass. Whew! She had gotten away with it.

"So ladies, we're all doing it! Jane is looking for the painting, Elle is dating, and I'm working out!" Chris cheered overly optimistically. She saw Jane's look of doubt.

"Yeah, ok," Jane began. "But really, Elle should be dating women and you should talk to Paul."

"And you should tell Dave how you feel," Chris added.

Jane responded quickly, "True, but I'm not ready yet so I'll find the painting and then I'll tell him and that will be good enough!"

Chris allowed it. If the conversation didn't end now, it may turn back to her and inevitably Frankie would come up. She wasn't ready for *that*.

The women wrapped up their evening, pledging to get together again soon.

Before bed, she turned back to her cellphone. She hadn't meant to keep Frankie waiting like that. But why was she communicating with this way-too-young man when she couldn't even communicate with her husband? But…she didn't want to leave him hanging. Afterall, *he* had reached out to *her*.

Hey you. Late girls' night. See you tomorrow. She added a kissy face emoji. Then deleted it. Then added it back and hit send.

CHAPTER NINE

The next day after work, per Angela's hunch, Jane walked into Fine Arts. It was yet another type of old haunt she hadn't visited in many years. She knew before arriving that finding clues about Ridgeley's whereabouts would be tough here. It was likely that most of the employees were college students or part-timers who'd been replaced many times over in the past fifteen years, but Jane still had to try.

Plus, she'd decided she should use this store visit as an opportunity. As much as she hated to admit it, the charcoal class had awakened something in her. She wasn't quite at the level of "opening up her storage shed and looking at old college shit," but she did miss the art world. It couldn't hurt to pick up just a few things in case inspiration struck, right?

"Can I help you?" a pink-haired, face-pierced Kyler asked her. She jumped, not expecting to deal with human contact right away.

"No, just looking. Thanks, Kyler."

"Uh, it's Brad," he responded, pointing to his name tag. It lied; he was *so* not a Brad, but whatever.

She sauntered past him and turned right. She'd need to do a full lap. Truth be told, she kind of wanted to do a full lap. As terrified as she was, there was a spark in her stomach that made her heart pound faster. She tasted faint notes of glitter and acrylic as she took in the store around her. Colored pencils filled the cylindric holes in rotating racks to her left. She'd always loved picking pencils. There were so many fun colors to choose from; so many more than the dark gray her life had felt like for a long time.

She snagged a teal pencil for good measure and kept walking, patting herself on the back for the great restraint she showed in not diving into the marker display. The smell of art supplies filled her nose like a subtle perfume. She allowed herself to run her hands over the rack of glossy paper to her right causing a tiny jolt to shoot through her stomach. She took in the sheets of stickers that somehow always tempted her no matter that she'd never put hearts or zoo animals on anything.

As Jane rounded the corner, her breath caught in her lungs. In front of her was an aisle that brought back memories: stacks and stacks of stretched canvas on panels to the right, and plain wood panels and hardboards to her left. Sure, some artists stretched their own canvases but Jane had never taken that plunge. Why do the overhead when she could just dive in to the part that exhilarated her? She used to stare at a blank canvas for hours at a time, envisioning the work she was about to create, mentally painting parts of it, leaving other parts a mystery for her brush to solve. She picked up a small stretched canvas and felt how taut the fabric was against the wood, yet it still had a bit of give. Just the right amount to allow the brush to dance with the canvas.

"Good lord," she muttered as she judged the cheesiness of her own thoughts. Problem was, she loved the passionately artistic cheesy stuff. She just hated that she loved it. Jane continued her walk down memory lane, or memory aisle, literally speaking. She made her way to the end and wrapped around the perimeter of the store, narrowly escaping another helpful employee. Jane passed easels, art bins, storage tubes, and portfolios.

Not quite ready for her true love, she moved to a close second: the soft pastels. Immediately drawn to a light pink oil pastel that shimmered, Jane touched the stick of color. Its loose powder rubbed onto her finger easily. She brushed it on the back of her hand as though she was testing a lip stick color. Bright shimmery glitter shone back. Instead of wiping it off, she left it there, proof of her bravery of making it to the store.

Realizing she had stalled long enough, Jane made a sharp decision and about faced, nearly colliding with the Kyler. "Can I help--" he began.

"Not yet Kyler. I need to get to the acrylics stat or I'll lose my nerve."

"It's Brad," he repeated under his breath as she speed-walked away from him. She turned the corner to enter the adjacent aisle and she almost threw up. In front of her was more acrylic paint than she'd need to cover the entire contents of the store. Jane had almost forgotten how much she loved the look of the tubes of paint, hanging by their tops, begging to be squeezed from the bottom so their cobalt blue or metallic silver could shoot triumphantly through the barrier and into the world where it belonged.

Mentally salivating, Jane shelved her fears and grabbed for the acrylics like her life depended on it. In a way, it did. "Damn it," she said aloud, as she again caught the poetic tone of her own thoughts. She grabbed various tubes of paint before realizing she didn't have a basket. Luckily, Kyler intervened and silently handed her one before she could panic. She dropped tube after tube into the basket, ultramarine blue, sapphire blue, cobalt blue, cerulean blue, cyan blue—really, way too many blues—and then a large tube of base white for mixing. She picked up some plastic egg trays and thought better of it. Those she still had in storage; she'd have to open it up once she got back to her apartment. Moving on to brushes, she immediately passed the synthetics and dove in to the natural whites. Jane loved the feel of a new paint brush: a bit rigid, a bit of bend, just like herself.

Ugh, she was drowning in her own floweriness. She had to get out of here before she fully crossed over into a patchouli-wearing, sage-burning disaster. She walked toward the checkout, Kyler trailing behind.

But wait! Ridgeley! She whirled around, startling her Kyler-shadow. "Excuse me. Can you introduce me to the person who has worked here the longest?" she asked him. He looked at her distrustfully, probably marking her as a weirdo. Which, given her behavior in the store, wasn't unexpected. "I'm trying to find someone who used to come here a lot a long time ago. She's an old…friend. I was hoping someone might remember her."

Kyler seemed appeased and took her to the back office. He introduced her to a man named Mel. Pleasantly gray-haired and pink-faced, Mel had worked there since the late 2000s. Given that she'd graduated in the mid-2000s, it was probable he hadn't met Ridgeley, but Jane showed him her drawing of Ridgeley anyway.

"Nope, can't say she looks familiar," he replied. Jane felt her heart plummet. Was this the end of it, then? "But...Kathryn's worked here since the late 90s. She retired not too long ago, but give me your number," he said, shuffling around for a pen, "and I'll have her call you. If Kathy feels comfortable about it, of course."

"That would be so great," Jane responded and rattled off her cell number. She made a mental note to answer her phone if an unknown number called.

Realizing she had gotten as far as she was going to get, Jane thanked him and returned to the front of the store, a shiver trickling down her spine. Not only was she one step closer to Ridgeley, but she was actually buying art supplies! She bee-lined to the register and Kyler rang her up in silence, only stating the total owed.

She grabbed the bag and took the receipt. Before exiting, Jane stopped and looked at him. "Thanks Brad," she said sincerely. He would never know how much he had helped, like a beacon of strength for Jane during her most trying task.

Just kidding. But he was cool and she did remember his real name.

She burst through the door a new woman. Or more of an older woman who had a closer touch to her past and her actual joy. She tried to hide a smile as she walked to her car. Not yet ready to discuss her triumph, but wanting a bit of credit she snapped a shot of her purchases and texted them to Christine. She waited only a few seconds before the tell-tale beep of a returned message came through. *Yayyyyyy!!!!!* Christine replied.

Yay indeed.

* * *

Christine was genuinely happy for her sister but the emotion was fleeting. Earlier that day she'd been picking up around the house. It was one thing to have to clean up after her kids, but Paul left his clothes strewn across the bedroom floor. As she picked up a pair of his pants, she noticed a folded post-it note fall out of the pocket. Picking it up, she read it before she realized what she was doing.

Those pants make you look yummy, it read.

What the fuck? First off, who handwrites a note? Send a text or an email like a civilized human being. Second, "yummy" is a word that toddlers use, not grown adults. Third, clearly this was from Angela. As she flipped the paper over, she saw her husband's handwriting.

Thanks, he had written.

Chris's head was spinning. Paul had replied to Angela's note, but the fact that it was in his possession meant he hadn't given it to her. Maybe they had a conversation about it instead? Or maybe they'd done something more about it. God, she had been talking a big game of his having an affair, but she'd been holding out hope that she was wrong. Here was his mistress, telling him how hot he looked. Proof in her hands. And Angela was right, he *did* look yummy in his tailored pants. Damn it! This is what such a note reduced her to: a woman speaking like a child. Her world shook.

Clearly, she and Paul needed to talk. But he was out golfing with his bosses today, so even if she wanted to, Christine couldn't confront him until later. And of course, by the time he got home she'd be exhausted from spending her Saturday morning cleaning the house, raising the kids, and prepping meals for her family.

Chris still didn't want to believe her husband was a cheater, even with the evidence mounting. She needed to confront him and get everything out in the open. But what if it was just harmless flirting? After all, he hadn't even replied in detail, just a "thanks," as if accepting a compliment. God knew she was guilty of the same.

A part of her realized she'd done more than the polite "thanks" with her own office romance. She thought about the zap of excitement and confidence she'd gotten from interacting with Frankie. If Paul had the same thing going, good on him. As long as their kids didn't find out, what was the harm really?

And if he truly was having an affair, then her texting Frankie was practically chaste. She grabbed her phone.

In case I haven't been clear, I think you're incredibly sexy. She didn't stop there.

I think about you in ways I shouldn't, she added.

Sexual ways. That had been clear, right?

What was she even *saying*? And just then, Cameron began to cry in the living room and Chris snapped out of flirtation mode and into Mommy mode.

It turns out Lucy had taken Cameron's favorite Lego, which was obviously a cry-able offense. She calmed her son down, retrieved the Lego, solicited an apology from Lucy, and began playing Legos with her kids. And it was a ton of fun.

This is what it was all about. Sure, Paul may be having an affair. But she needed to stay focused on her family. Lucy and Cameron were everything to her. They were everything to Paul too, though he may have forgotten that as of late. She could remind him. He would appreciate that. After all, they were a family.

Tonight, she and Paul would talk. A *real* talk. They'd lay it all out (not that she had much dirty laundry to air), and they'd reconnect.

The kids' bedtime came around. She tucked her little ones in and waited on the couch for Paul. An hour passed. *Where was he?*

Another hour passed and she grabbed her phone to text him. *When are you coming home?*

Sorry. Really late tonight.

God damnit.

And that's when she saw it. The message from Frankie.

Damn, Chris, look how excited you got me. With a picture of his excitement. His very big excitement.

She practically dropped her phone. It was incredible. And she had caused it.

* * *

Elle logged into Facebook and saw that she had three notifications, one of which made her smile immediately. It was a friend request from a guy she knew from her office building, though he didn't work at the center. Well, "knew" was a strong word. They'd had a few interactions, and he was friendly with Beth, a receptionist at the center. Elle would never forget the time he brought a kid into the center that he'd met on the street. The boy had been living on the streets in Kevin's neighborhood and he thought the kid might benefit from the center. That was a classy move.

Looking at his picture, Elle noticed Kevin was actually pretty good looking in sort of a gray-haired Vince Vaughn way. She checked his age. Hmm, thirty-seven. Well, if his hair was that gray at thirty-seven, he must have been through some things in life. That was a plus. Besides, he wasn't one of those guys trying to look younger by dying his hair (sure, Elle dyed hers but that wasn't about *age* it was about *style*). They guy wasn't afraid to be himself, had a steady job, and they knew some of the same people so he couldn't be a total psychopath. Interesting.

After Tom, Elle briefly considered dating women again. Jane had certainly been nagging her to. But thoughts of Lilly made her hesitant. After all, she knew where that road led.

As she accepted the friend request, she noticed Kevin had liked a few of her more recent photos, so she went to his page and liked something back. If she was going to date in the age of social media, she might as well do it like the kids did. While on his page, she did a bit of digging. He had no relationship status listed, which was a plus. His pictures included a few photos of him hugging a pretty girl. Girlfriend? She clicked on them to check the dates. Nope, they were all from at least two years ago so, given his lack of status, they had probably broken up.

About thirty minutes later she received a message from Kevin. *Fancy meeting you here.*

I am pretty fancy, she replied.

The brief interaction put a smile on her face; any potential romantic connection felt like a good thing.

Later that night, he responded. *I can't argue with that, m'lady.*

Elle blushed, despite herself. Well, she wasn't much of a blusher but she assumed this was what blushing felt like. It wasn't a particularly deep message, but it was sweet and she liked it. She checked herself. Did she like *him?* She needed to know more about him, but the good thing was he wasn't a stranger from an app.

Her previous strategy of gathering the information for her list right away hadn't been working that well. And she didn't want to jump right to "wanna be my baby-daddy?" That info could reveal itself over time. Since he had taken most of the day to respond, she decided she should keep it chill.

Her phone pinged from a message from Jane. Apparently, she wanted Elle to come over and didn't even care if she had to supply the alcohol. Knowing a win-win when she saw it, Elle walked toward Jane's to spend the rest of her evening watching stupid television.

She burst in Jane's door with energy she didn't even know she had.

"Girrrrl," Elle practically shouted.

"Whoa. What's with the excitement?" Jane questioned.

"I have a lead. I *may* be able to ditch dating apps!"

"Well that was sudden. What's up?"

She filled Jane in on Kevin, knowing that from now on Jane would only refer to him as Gray-Haired Vince Vaughn.

"I mean, it could have potential. How do you feel about working in the same building?"

Elle considered this. Dating someone she knew from real life had ups and downs.

"I mean, good and bad. He's not a complete stranger..."

"So he's less likely to be stalky, like Tom," Jane finished the thought.

"Right, and we know at least some of the same people so he has context in my life."

"Fair."

"But if things went south...Oh God, I'd still have to run into him. And make small talk. And be civil." Elle briskly ran her fingers through her hair. "Fuck."

Jane piped up. "Ok dude, I think you're getting a bit ahead of yourself. I mean no offense but you're not dating. You've had, like, one text exchange."

Shit. Jane was right. She was getting *way* ahead of herself. What was her problem?

"It seems like this baby fever has got you fucked up. Like, you're just on a mission. You barely know this guy so you don't even know if you'll like him."

Ok, fair point. But he was still a better option than dating apps! An optimistic Elle logged into Facebook and *bam*! A message from Kevin.

How's life at the center?

"He messaged me again," she updated Jane.

"Cool. But Elle, I'm just saying, you don't know him. You're just trying to fast-forward to settling down and it doesn't work like that. Also, you need to date women."

There she went *again*! Why was Jane so set on her dating women? She was *bisexual* and not *gay*. There was a difference. Sure, her only successful relationship had been with a woman, and yeah sexuality was a spectrum and she was better at opening up to women but *still*. She wanted a fucking *baby!* It was much easier to make one with a man.

Enough about this. Elle changed the topic. "Ok. I'm done with this. What's up with you?"

Jane filled Elle in on her excursion to Fine Arts. Despite her

127

annoyance at her best friend, Elle was pretty proud that Jane was getting back into art.

"I even bought some supplies," Jane said, hesitating. "Not like I'm gonna use them."

"But at least you have the option," Elle replied.

Options. That's exactly what she needed but time was running out. Fuck. She really hoped something would happen with Kevin. This whole dating thing sucked.

CHAPTER TEN

After Elle left, Jane was still energized. She wished her friend would have stayed longer but Elle was in a mood. Jane grabbed her phone and texted Dave to fill him in on her excursion to Fine Art. It was weird that it felt so natural reaching out to her old best friend. Who she still had feelings for.

Again, he responded immediately. *Janey, I'm proud of you. You went to an art class and a store! Let's hang again soon.*

Jane swooned so hard she practically fell off of her chair. She obviously wanted to see Dave again and couldn't believe he wanted to see her too. But with all of these memories coming back to her through her Ridgeley hunt, she needed to get her mind together.

Over the past few weeks she'd been to an art museum, taken

an art class, and purchased supplies, including *acrylics*. And in a way, she'd done this *because* of Ridgeley. The very woman she'd blamed for taking art away from her. She thought back to that day. Competition day. Ridgeley hadn't been wretched and awful. She'd told Jane her painting was amazing and should've won. And she asked to have it. Did that sound like someone trying to make Jane quit art?

Fuck. It hit Jane like a ton of bricks. Ridgeley was never wretched and awful to *Jane*, Jane was wretched and awful to *her*. She had been a jealous, immature child who lost, and so took her ball and went home. Welp. Hopefully, she'd have the opportunity to apologize to Ridgeley in the near future.

And yeah, Jane had left Dave. She'd already come to grips with that. But thank God he was back in her life. And she was going to see him again soon!

Relaxing, Jane tried to watch more TV, but the Fine Art materials she had purchased sat in a bag in her living room and itched at her mind. A twitch in her fingers finally made her stand up and walk over to the bag. What was she doing? Whatever, this wasn't a commitment. If she played around with some paint or pastels it didn't mean she was re-entering the art world. No! She was alone in her apartment with nothing to do, so why not? This wasn't a big deal. She wasn't ready for acrylics, but she could play around with the other stuff.

She reached in and took out the sketch pad she had purchased, plus one of the shimmery pink pastels. What was it with this color? Jane wasn't much of a pink girl, in aesthetic or personality, but somehow this pink made her feel light inside. She sighed slightly as the pastel hit the paper. Kind of like the sigh you make when you wade into a warm pool of water.

Ugh, the cheese. *Stop it, Jane.*

The color had been tainted a bit with a former neighboring cobalt blue pastel, but that only made it more of a delight to spread across the page.

Well shit, she'd better just give in to the cheesiness.

Feeling the soft smoosh of the powder hitting paper made Jane feel like an adult revisiting an old elementary school classroom. Such beautiful nostalgia. She allowed her finger to rub the thick coarse lines she had made on the sketch pad to smooth them out and blend the shimmer. She glanced at her finger. She noted the perfection of her now pink finger print and did something she used to do. She ran her pastel-covered finger along both cheeks to give herself an 80's-esque new wave look. Jane giggled as she remembered doing this as a young girl at her kitchen table.

Back to the drawing. She turned on some music and allowed herself to get lost. A moment of panic struck when she took her head out of the game. Her stomach froze. Oh God, what did this all mean? Nothing, it wasn't a big deal. She was just playing around with pastels. She took a sip of wine and when Fleetwood Mac's "Gypsy" started playing out of her stereo, she was back in.

After about twenty minutes she evaluated her work. *Play.* Not work, play! It was pretty cool. She had created a landscape with a blazing sun and some avant-garde, Tim Burton-like trees all in shimmery pink, giving the world a fairy-dusted appearance. It was fun, but it was missing something.

She reached back into her bag of goodies and pulled out a charcoal stick. The stick had a slightly glazed casing, kind of like the good chalk for chalkboards in elementary school. She added in some shading and light lines to her trees and some other swizzles of gray and black to make the landscape pop, and to add a tone of darkness and edge to the otherwise fairy-like world. Ahh, much better.

Jane hung the picture on her refrigerator, because that's what you do with fun drawings that are not work and are only for fun. She sat back down, feeling a release in her stomach and picked up her wine glass, leaving black and pink finger prints on it.

She thought of texting a picture of it to Christine. But, ugh. Chris would be all excited about it and make it into a big deal. *Which it wasn't!* Elle was in a funk so she wasn't sending it to her. But maybe it'd cheer her up? Now *Jane* was making it into a big deal. But if it wasn't one, then why couldn't she send it to her closest friends?

That settled it. Without a further thought, she snapped a shot of her work (*play!*) and texted it to Chris and Elle. And Dave.

Holding her breath, she jumped up when Christine responded.

Oh Jane. It's beautiful.

Hell yeah, Elle joined in.

Jane felt a tear coming to her eye. She looked at her drawing. It really was beautiful. Her phone pinged again.

Jane, you've still got it, Dave stated simply.

Jane screenshot his text and sent it to Elle and Chris. I mean, the cat was already out of the bag. They knew she was into him.

Elle responded, *Meet up with him again, bitch!*

* * *

Elle, sitting at her desk, filling out a progress report on one of her teens, heard a ping. Looking down, she noticed a Facebook notification. Huh, an event invite. Apparently, it was Kevin's birthday this weekend and Elle had officially been invited to his party. This bode well for his being interested in her. The party was at a restaurant with a dance party afterward. Ok, not her vibe but still, Beth from the center already responded yes so at least Elle would know someone there. Elle was in!

After all, if she wanted to get to know Kevin better, she needed to make an effort to hang out outside of the office and work functions.

She took a minute to look at the other event accepters. Stranger, stranger, that guy was from the building, stranger, someone else from the building. Ooh, *hello* hot woman. Nope, she couldn't get distracted. She was here for Kevin. Ok, so she'd know a few people at the event. Even better.

That night, while hanging out in her apartment, Elle's phone dinged with a Facebook message.

Stoked you're coming on Saturday! Kevin had written. Elle rechecked the event invite. He was turning thirty-eight, one year older than her.

Happy birthday! What's it like to be so old?

Guess I'll find out Saturday! he replied.

Come Saturday, Elle texted Beth to confirm she was going. They agreed to meet for a pre-party drink at another bar down the street. They also agreed to wait out dinner and only join for the after-food festivities (though Elle would *not* be dancing).

Once they got their drinks—Elle's usual whiskey neat, Beth a margarita—they chatted about work and how it felt impossible to make a dent in the field of social work. At a lull in conversation, Beth turned to Elle.

"So, are you and Kevin close?"

"Not at all. I've just seen him around the office. I don't know him very well."

"Oh. I was thinking you might be friends with Mary."

"Who's Mary?" Elle asked.

"Kevin's girlfriend."

Oh, shit. He *did* have a girlfriend. In fact, wasn't Mary the name of the girl in the photos from two years ago? Was she his long-term and very current girlfriend? A better question was why the hell had he messaged Elle out of the blue when he was in a relationship?

She had come too far to turn back now. Plus, she and Beth were not close enough for her to admit that she wanted to leave because Kevin wasn't single. As they closed out their tabs, Elle put on her big-girl face and they walked to the party spot.

Kevin's face lit up as he took Elle in, his eyes roving once over her, then doing a slow up-and-down. Had he just checked her out? His grin was suggestive. Yes, he had definitely just checked her out, which seemed shady as hell for a guy she only kind of knew. Particularly for a guy. With. A. Girlfriend!

Deciding she wanted nothing to do with Kevin's current vibe, she grabbed a drink and posted up a good fifty feet away from him.

Elle decided forty-five minutes was the magical amount of time she'd need to spend at the party without eliciting any unwanted questions about an early departure from Beth. She passed the time by chatting with some strangers about differences between whiskey, bourbon, and scotch, and avoiding the dance floor at all costs. She glanced around the room for the hot girl from the invite, but she wasn't there. Typical L.A. flakiness. Bummer.

About twenty minutes into her sentence at the party, she heard a male voice over the microphone. It was Kevin, about to make a "thanks for coming to my birthday" announcement. Elle turned politely to face the birthday boy. After various cheers from his raucous friends, he called Mary over. Thanking her for planning the party and bringing a cake, he turned to his girlfriend.

"These past 2 years have been the best of my life, and all because of you. Mary…" Kevin suddenly took a knee. Holy fucking shit, he was proposing! Elle barely knew this couple and yet she was at their engagement.

"…Will you marry me?"

Fucking hell.

"YES!" Mary shouted and the room erupted as the newly engaged couple shared a kiss that made Elle roll her eyes. Did they have to do that in front of all the single people who unknowingly and unwillingly were now a part of this engagement celebration?

Elle downed her drink and decided she didn't give a fuck what kinds of questions Beth may have for her. She was out of there.

As she walked out the door, Kevin caught her eye for a split second. She saluted for lack of a better gesture—and not with her middle finger like she was itching to do.

This whole endeavor was a nightmare. And really, what in the fuck was Kevin doing in the first place? Elle would check around, but she was fairly certain that sending direct messages to an almost stranger was not something one did in a non-flirtatious way. When she got home, she pulled out her list and added a bullet point: *Single!*

* * *

Christine handed Elle another whiskey as she re-told the saga from the night before.

"Fuck that bullshit," Jane offered.

Christine agreed, and added a bit more. "It sounds like he wanted one last hurrah before he committed."

"You think?" Elle asked.

Chris elaborated. "Not physically. I mean, he didn't actually try to cheat. He hadn't tried to meet up with you, right?"

"Correct," confirmed Elle.

"Maybe he wanted to feel that twinge of desiring and being desired by another woman before locking it down for the rest of his life."

"Fuck that bullshit!" Jane offered again, this time more emphatically.

"Well, I kind of get it. There's nothing wrong with a bit of harmless flirting, as long as nobody got hurt," Christine continued, nonchalantly. She immediately noticed Elle and Jane connect eyes in a "what was *that*" kind of way. *Shit!*

"It's true! I have friends that have done it." She hoped that diversion worked. Just in case, she poured each another drink. Maybe they wouldn't remember their suspicions!

After a bit of conversation about Jane's trip to the art supply store, Elle piped back up.

"Chris, you're right. Kevin probably just wanted a final flirtation before taking the plunge with his real-life girlfriend. I get it, but that's not cool. To her or to me."

"No, it isn't, but you barely know him. *Fuck* him," Jane said. "Elle. I'm sorry, but I think it's time. You need to date women. You like them more than men." She looked at Elle with serious-face; Elle looked down, avoiding eye-contact. "I know you're thirty-seven and you feel like you need to get knocked up right now or the chance will go away. But it's not true."

"Oh, honey, I think Jane is right," Chris wanted to hug Elle, but knew it wouldn't be appreciated.

In an uncharacteristic move, Elle looked almost on the verge of tears. "What do I do? What the fuck do I do?"

Chris had this one. She wasn't sure why Elle hadn't come up with it on her own. "Freeze your eggs," she offered simply. "I don't know if you've ever really considered the idea, but maybe it's time you do."

"Shit." Downing the rest of her whiskey, Elle continued. "You know, in the past I always figured having kids would happen or it wouldn't. And I'd be fine either way. So I never really thought about that."

"And now?" Chris and Jane asked simultaneously.

"I don't know. I mean, it sounds kind of crazy to me. I never thought I'd need high science to procreate. But shit."

Chris could see that Elle could use a release of the pressure valve that was pulling at her insides. She squeezed Chris's shoulders, communicating that she'd give this some serious thought.

Later that night, Chris got a text from Jane. *What the fuck was that comment about flirting? What's going on with you? You're not doing anything stupid, are you?*

Christine didn't answer.

For Chris, the next few days went by without incident. She and Frankie texted back and forth a bit, but it was nothing she wouldn't want Paul to see. It was as if he'd sensed he'd taken it too far with his last 'message.' *Not that she hadn't appreciated it.* He stopped by her office a few times and she visited his cubicle. They exchanged a smile when a co-worker mentioned something about Cable's Bar and Grille. Chris wasn't sure what to make of this return to friendship but felt the loss of the sexual tension she'd come to relish.

On Friday, Chris found herself working late. She'd realized

by lunchtime that she wasn't going to get home on time and made arrangements for Jane to watch the kids. Paul verified he'd be home by seven, so Chris didn't feel so bad about commandeering her sister to play babysitter.

She was lost in her computer when Frankie knocked on her door around six-thirty.

"What are you still doing here on a Friday night?" he asked playfully.

"Trying to wrap things up with this property. What about you? Shouldn't you be out doing something fun or…something?" She stumbled a bit as she tried to pull her head out of work mode.

"I'm here doing something fun," he joked. "Want to go grab a drink when you're done, or do you need to get going?"

Christine fought against every inch of herself that was screaming *hell yes.*

"I really shouldn't," she hedged.

"Oh, ok. Cool," he replied. Chris detected disappointment, but appreciated that Frankie was respectful.

He walked away and she tried furiously to wrap up work. Finally, she was able to send off the documents to the escrow company. As she stood to walk out of the office, her phone buzzed. Paul. *Things crazy at work. Won't be home til 9:30 or later. Sorry.*

Un-fucking-believable. Here she was, playing friendly with her office crush *who was nothing more than a crush* and her husband was at it again. Yeah, she knew things had gotten out of hand over text with Frankie. But Paul was probably neck deep into Angela at this very moment.

Chris shuddered at the thought. She had never, *would never,* take it physical with Frankie. But you know what? Right now, she didn't give a fuck if grabbing a drink with him was crossing the line. Frankie had backed off after taking his texting too far, so obviously boundaries could be set. *They could actually be friends.* And it was time to do something for herself. If that that something was grabbing a drink with a friend who made her feel sexy and *seen,* so fucking what?

Chris texted her sister. *You cool to stay til like 9:30?*

Yep, Jane replied immediately, followed by, *Killing it* and a pic of her and the kids in full make-up, Cam included.

Chris raced to Frankie's cubicle, hoping to God he was still there. She rolled up slightly out of breath, more out of anxiousness than the workout of the 100-yard walk.

"You still up for that drink?" she asked.

He looked surprised, but then that million-watt grin took over his face. "Yeah, of course," he replied.

Yes!

Frankie picked a different bar this time. It was a quiet place, dark and sexy. Red pleather booths, dank carpeting, barely brighter than candlelit.

It felt like a place a woman would go to cheat on her husband.

Chris moved to grab a seat at the bar and Frankie lightly touched her arm. "I was thinking we could get a table. If you're hungry at all."

"Oh, ok sure," she replied. She *was* hungry and what was a bit of food in a sexy cheater's bar amongst friends?

They ordered drinks from the waitress and nibbled on bread as they perused the menu.

"So, what are you thinking?" Chris asked, her eyes skimming over the entrees.

"Honestly, I'm thinking about you."

She jerked up to find his gaze on her, dark and intense. "I meant for dinner," she clarified.

"So did I."

Whoa. Chris downed her glass of water.

"Oh my God, I'm so sorry. I took that way too far again. Fuck." He seemed genuinely embarrassed.

"No. Well yes. I mean, I'd be lying if I said I didn't enjoy hearing you talk like that about me, but I'm a married woman. With two kids." And with that, Chris's boundary was set. She felt a bit of pride that she had done the right thing and chosen family first. To save them both the embarrassment, she should go. Really. Yet, she wasn't leaving.

"So, tell me more about yourself. What do you do when you're not in the office? How does a good-looking guy like you, no kids, not a care in the world spend his time?" she asked. Ok, so the boundary wasn't perfect. And she was clearly trying to find out if he was dating. But they weren't talking about fucking, which felt like a win.

"I surf a lot. I have a great group of friends I hang out with. And no. I'm not dating anyone."

Chris choked on her wine. *Damn.* She thought she had been more subtle than *that!*

Topic change. "Tell me about your friends. What do you guys do for fun? And what drew you to real estate?" Ok. Those were actually neutral questions.

Frankie answered her questions with the perfect amount of detail, and asked about her as well. Christine felt like she was genuinely getting to know this man; this ridiculously enticing, muscular, sweet young man. It struck her as strange that he clearly wanted to know her as well. She didn't understand what he saw in her, but she believed him when he said that he couldn't stop thinking about her. She shifted her legs with intention. She needed to control herself. She had already dodged the sex-talk bullet, but that didn't mean she was safe from her own desires.

As dinner wrapped up, Frankie insisted on grabbing the check. "It's the least I can do after my inappropriate comment."

It was sweet he was still calling it inappropriate, particularly since, the more Christine thought about it, the more it turned her on.

He walked her to her car, their arms centimeters from brushing. This was not the distance two friends kept between them. As they arrived at her car, Chris looked into Frankie's eyes and what came next felt so natural she barely had time to stop herself. She grabbed his collar and leaned in to kiss him on the mouth.

"Are you sure?" he whispered.

Christine paused. She was not actually sure of anything. "You're right. I can't."

"I understand," Frankie said as he took a half step back.

Chris panicked at the distance and pulled him back in. Sparks filled her intestines. His tongue filled her mouth, the perfect depth. Not too much. She felt like a college kid. Ravenously, back and forth. Devouring each other, her head tossing back in ecstasy. His hands running over her face. Then down, over her shoulders and—*Fuck! What was she doing?*

Chris pulled away with a force. "I . . . I can't do this. I'm so sorry."

"Fuck. I'm sorry too," a panting Frankie looked genuinely regretful.

"No, Frankie, you didn't do it. We did. I did. But I can't. I can't ever again."

With that, she slunk into her car and locked the door. Without looking back, she drove away from the giant mistake she had just made.

A tear rolled down her cheek. As she drove home, she promised herself she'd admit everything to Jane. She needed a friend and no one was closer to her than her sister. She knew Jane would get a bit judgey at first, but she would check herself and listen once Christine made her needs known. Ok. It was all going to be ok.

As she pulled into her driveway and opened the garage door, she saw Paul's car there. Fuck. If he was home, she couldn't talk to Jane. Chris buried the mess of emotion in her stomach, straightened up, and walked into her house as though it were any typical evening. She could play the role of normal, loving wife rather than emotional and slightly physical cheater.

"¡Hola mi hermana!" Jane said as she walked in the door. She and Paul were sitting on the couch sipping wine, probably talking about sports or something banal. As Paul stood to greet her, Christine froze. What the fuck had she done?

"Hi baby," he said as approached, coming for a kiss. Chris turned her head instinctively. She couldn't have Paul kiss her lips with residue from Frankie's still on them.

Paul kissed her cheek and ruffled her hair, not having noticed her avoidance of full-on lip contact.

"I'll get you a glass of wine," he added.

"Awww, yeah!" Jane approved.

And it all seemed so normal. Sure, Paul hadn't been around much lately but was he acting like a man who was cheating? She had only kissed someone and was completely losing her mind. If he was actually *fucking* someone else, would he have stood to kiss

142

her? Would he be hanging out with her sister? *Oh God.* Maybe he *wasn't* cheating. Suddenly, this option was infinitely worse.

She was the cheater. She had stepped out on *him.* That was true regardless. Though really, she had only *kissed* Frankie. It wasn't *that* bad. But it wasn't good. Had she made up the story about Paul's cheating to give herself permission to do the same? At this point, she had no clue.

"I'll be back in a minute," she said back weakly. She immediately went upstairs to kiss her sleeping kids goodnight, though she barely felt she deserved to do so.

As she kissed Lucy and Cam on their foreheads, she made up her mind. That was it. What had barely begun with Frankie was over. She would not do this to her family.

CHAPTER ELEVEN

Jane woke to a loud ringing, causing her to jump up from bed. *8:30.* Who the hell calls people at 8:30 in the morning? She didn't recognize the number but realized the call could be Ridgeley-related. Reluctant to commit to the phone call until she knew who it was, she hit answer and said nothing. After a few seconds she heard a weak, "Hello?"

"Hello," Jane whispered back quickly, as though she could get out of this more easily if she barely spoke.

"This is Kathryn from Fine Art calling for Jane?" the woman half stated, half asked.

"Oh, hi!" Jane said, now speaking like a normal person. "Thanks so much for calling. I was hoping to talk to you about someone who used to come into Fine Art."

"I'd be happy to!"

"Great! She went by Ridgeley. She would've last been in..."
"Oh, actually, I think this might be easier to do in person. No?" Kathryn added.

"Um, why's that?"

"Well that way we'll have time for you to give me all the details and see if you can jog my memory."

Jane would obviously prefer to do it over the phone, but Kathryn did have a point. Jane could show her the drawing and the cat signature if she saw her face-to-face.

"Yes, you're absolutely right," Jane recovered. "Are you by any chance free today at around six?"

"Six would be fine," Kathryn agreed easily.

They agreed to meet at a coffee shop near Kathryn's house, and Jane got ready for work.

At around ten, Jane rolled into Hudson. One thing she absolutely adored about working in market research for Hudson Solutions was that nobody cared about the petty things like arrival time. Well, no one except for Todd, who raised his eyebrows and looked at his watch exaggeratedly as Jane walked by. Fuck Todd. At Hudson, employees were free to come and go as they pleased and to wear whatever they wanted (within reason) as long as the work was done. In fact, a representative from HR wore a different cat themed sweatshirt every day of the week, on a perfectly repeated rotation Monday through Friday.

Jane's office was decorated much like her home, only here she felt a little more free to hang the art that inspired her. She didn't go so far as to adorn the walls with any of her own work; she wouldn't want it contaminated with the corporate bullshit that seeped from the walls. Plus, a deeply rooted knot in her stomach had always tightened whenever she thought of going into her storage unit at home and pulling out her old stuff.

She sat down at her desk, turned on her unnecessary-due-to-fluorescent-ceiling-lights desk lamp and logged into her computer. A minute or so later, Jane began scrolling through her emails. 146 new messages. Ugh. When people asked her what she did for a living, she often said she was a professional emailer and left it at that. Then again, who wasn't a professional emailer these days?

Jane drifted through her day, accomplishing less than she should have, until around six when she headed out to meet up with Kathryn from Fine Art.

Jane recognized the woman immediately; her voice over the phone had instantly telegraphed her appearance and she was exactly as Jane had pictured with thinning gray hair and a somewhat frumpy t-shirt (no offense, Kathryn). They sat down for a bit and Jane immediately understood that Kathy would have met up with anyone willing to talk about art at length. She seemed to not remember that Jane had a specific reason for coming and went off on long tangents about trends in the art world and upcoming shows. Eventually, Jane found a second to intervene. She showed her the picture of Ridgeley and Kathy studied it for a few minutes.

"You know, I think I do remember her. She used to call me Counselor."

"Really?" Jane asked excitedly. Then she squinted, adding, "Why?"

"Well, she had gone to some art camp as a child and one day she approached me asking if I was one of the teachers from the camp. I wasn't, but from then on it was our inside joke. She'd see me all the time and her nickname for me was Counselor."

More clues into the mysterious life of Ridgeley. Unfortunately, there were hundreds of art camps around Los Angeles. Jane drilled Kathy for any other tidbits of information she might have but the well had run dry. The poor woman looked upset when Jane said she had to go. Jane sat back down. Kathy had agreed to meet up with her, and she wasn't creepy; she simply wanted to talk about art. Jane ordered them another round of coffees and they chatted for another hour before parting ways.

On her way home, Jane texted Dave. *One step closer...* she typed.

As she waited for a reply, she checked her phone constantly. Dave usually responded so quickly. Where was he? What was he doing? *He has a life, dumbass.* Right. He could be doing anything. But that was the problem. She wanted him to be with her. Only, how could she expect to spend time with him when she hadn't asked him to? Hell, she hadn't even been responsive when he'd offered. What was wrong with her? Looking for Ridgeley was helping her get off her ass in general. It was time she got off her ass about Dave too. What was the worst that could happen, inviting Dave further into her life? He had been there before. *Had he been there the whole time?* No he hadn't, thanks to Jane's insecurity. But maybe he should have been.

She texted again. *Wanna hang for a bit?*

About twenty minutes later her phone dinged.

I can hang in about an hour and a half. That work?

That worked.

Jane texted him her address. It felt only natural to invite her friend to her home, which he had never seen.

Ninety minutes later, Jane practically threw her apartment door open with an enthusiastic, "Welcome to my humble abode."

Dave cracked a heat-emitting grin that warmed Jane up and thawed some of her nerves.

"Wow," he started. *Yes!* He liked her place. "You have no art on your walls," he finished.

Seeing her face drop, Dave added, "It's a really great place though! I'm just, surprised."

Of course he was surprised! The last place of Jane's he'd seen was her sophomore dorm room, with walls covered in her own work and pieces that inspired it. Her dorm was basically a low-rent museum. Hmm. Her roommate must have hated that. Oh well.

She cleared her throat. "Yeah, I haven't ... I mean, you know ... hadn't done much since college."

"Oh. I was wrong. There's this! Janey, it's a start!" Dave pulled her recent pastel creation off of the fridge to examine it closer. "It's even better in person. You've still got the same style." He really did know her. "God, you're so good."

Not quite knowing what to say next, Jane went with what she knew best. "Want a drink?"

"Sure," Dave answered easily. He was always so easy. Why was she tense?

"Remember in your dorm, that painting you had from high school of a sunny windstorm?"

She had forgotten about that! "Oh my God, yes! A senior year assignment of 'juxtaposition.' I think that might be in my storage downstairs."

"Let's go find out."

Jane froze. Was she ready to fully open her past? With Dave by her side, there was no better time. Fuck it!

"Ok," Jane acquiesced. Dave looked amused. He clearly hadn't expected a yes.

They went to the parking garage and Jane paused. Dave squeezed her shoulder, knowing this was big for her. And with that, Jane unlocked the storage unit and leaned in to what she feared. *And it was fucking awesome!* Tons of art stuff from college, pictures she had drawn, paintings, charcoals. Dave remembered most of them as much as she did.

"Oh my God, this is that one you did freshman year about adulthood."

Jane laughed. "And this is the drawing I did of your foot. Remember that?" Now Dave was laughing. "Whoa, I did a charcoal of Stevie Nicks?"

"You don't remember that? I remember that." Dave added, "And holy shit, it's the sunny windstorm from high school." So it *was* still in her storage.

Not quite ready to adorn her walls with her entire art history, Jane grabbed the windstorm.

"Let's go hang this, shall we?" she smiled.

"Hell yes," Dave agreed. They put the rest back in storage, though Jane made a mental note to pick up a few more later. She grabbed a couple of acrylics supplies too, just in case, and went back upstairs.

Choosing the perfect place in the middle of her living room wall, Dave hammered in a nail as Jane hung the painting. She held in a tear as she saw the beauty of this moment. She didn't even have the energy to judge that thought.

Returning to their drinks, Jane and Dave chatted an hour away without even feeling the passage of time. Eventually, Dave asked Jane how the search for Ridgeley was coming along.

Once she mentioned the part about camp, Dave stood up. "Holy shit Janey! I remember that! She drove me past that place and said she used to go there. I remember where it was."

"No way!"

"I totally do. I remember because after we drove past it we had a super-hot makeout sesh."

Jane's head snapped toward Dave. There was that sheepish grin. The *fucker!*

"Just kidding. But I do remember it," Dave said, beginning to draw a map. How adorably archaic! And after she had completely boxed him out of her life in college, here he was, in her adult apartment, handing her the next step in her journey.

Dave had an early morning the next day, so after finishing the map he had to leave. Jane, thanking him profusely, walked him to the door.

"Aw, Janey, you're welcome," he said sincerely, moving in for a bear hug. Jane wrapped her arms around him tightly.

And seconds passed. Was this the normal length of a hug? Did it mean something more? Neither was letting go. But they were old friends so it made sense. Or did it? Not knowing what to do, Jane squeezed Dave's shoulder and he broke the embrace. Fuck!

After he left, Jane poured herself another glass of wine and looked at her wall. The painting looked right at home.

She sat down and grabbed her phone, texting Elle.

Might have just had a sexually tense moment with Dave. Hang soon to analyze.

* * *

Elle sat in her apartment, completely over the dating scene. App dating had proven a bust and so did meeting men IRL. Jane might be right that she needed to consider dating women again, but she wasn't sure she was ready. What she really needed was a break.

Instead of focusing on dating, maybe she should focus on making new friends. Expanding her circle would force her to cross paths with people she otherwise wouldn't have met, which couldn't hurt. She loved Jane and Chris, but her life outside of work did feel a bit insular. But how could she meet people?

She sat for a few minutes until lightning struck. It was so obvious. *How had she not thought of it before?* She spent half of her free time exploring different parts of the city, dives, taquerías, whatever. She was such a natural loner, she had never even thought to just talk casually to people at these places. *Duh.* Elle had always kept sex and city time completely separate. It was time for that to change.

Fuck it, Elle thought. It was nine on a Saturday and she felt like going out. She threw on her leather jacket and black boots, grabbed her phone, and headed for the door. She was going on an adventure, but this time she was making friends! Hooking-up she could do with her eyes closed, but trying to create friendships? Well, outside Jane it had been a while.

As she headed out the door, her phone buzzed. It was a text from Jane, a picture of a wineglass with a question mark. Nah. She was committed to her plan. She texted back, *Sorry kid,* and went on her way. Her phone buzzed once more and she smiled as she saw

Jane's thumbs down emoji response. Knowing the conversation was over, she threw her phone in her pocket and headed to the train station.

Instead of heading downtown, she went toward Hollywood. Hollywood had the perfect mix of outcasts and in-casts that would make her feel at home, with the added benefit of it being an absolute hub for women going out on the town. Not necessarily gay or bisexual women, but tonight wasn't about that.

Standing outside the W, Elle was tempted to hang out with a drugged-up guy talking about the end of days. But that friendship wouldn't last. Instead, she walked toward a group of 30-something women and asked if they knew of a good place to grab a whiskey. She explained that she was a local but didn't get to Hollywood much and wanted to check it out. They chatted for a bit, each party deeming the other harmless. After a few minutes, the ladies mentioned they were going to a bar and invited Elle to tag along.

She had no designs on these women. They were clearly straight and not her type. But this was exactly what she was aiming for: friends!

She accepted the invitation without a second thought and braced herself for a night of randomness. Elle's fear that she wouldn't pass the dress code of wherever the girls were going was quickly abated. They had chosen the bar at a comedy club; one of their friends was performing in a show later that night and they were going to support her.

Elle got herself a whiskey neat, then joined the women at their table. As she settled in she asked the usual friend-making questions (she knew what they were, she just didn't usually care): jobs, hobbies, where they were originally from, what brought them to L.A. It was the first time in a long time that she had spoken with perfect strangers she had nothing in common with; these were the kind of people that Jane would have written off immediately as pumpkin spice latte drinkers (which they probably were). And shit, it was kind of fun.

The friend's stand-up routine was surprisingly legit. Elle knew enough about her city to know that seeing a friend do comedy could be hit or miss. The jokes were topical and focused on the absurdities of fad diets: calories being a 90s thing, kale having a great PR person, the war against gluten. Elle found herself laughing out loud, something she rarely did. And to think she never even would have come here save for her encounter with these women. It really validated her plan to just get out and talk to strangers.

After the show, she thanked them for an awesome night out. Amber, the one who was a bartender and originally from New York, gave Elle her email address and Insta handle so she could get the pics. She also told Elle about an upcoming party the following weekend. "It'd be great if you could make it!" she gushed.

Elle's initial instinct was to bail on the invite, but then she remembered the entire point of the evening. "I'm in," she replied. Hell, maybe she'd actually go.

The next night, Elle wanted to help Jane celebrate her success—both the new Ridgeley info and the was-that-hug-too-long-in-a-good-way thing with Dave—so they decided to meet up and head to K.C.'s.

Walking in, the scan for the perfect table commenced. As her eyes adjusted to the dimly lit bar, Elle stopped in her tracks.

Lilly.

Lilly was here, in *her* bar. With another woman. It was a bit disrespectful of Lilly to come to her ex's regular hang out with a new girlfriend. But hey, free country and whatnot.

"Oh shit," she heard Jane whisper as the memories poured over Elle, pulling her into the past.

At the age of thirty-two, Elle had fallen for Lilly hard and fast. Though Elle wasn't exactly an expert in the world of relationships, she had much more experience than Lilly, who was six years her junior. In fact, Elle was the first person Lilly had seriously dated.

Lilly was the kind of girl that felt everything. Elle was drawn to her because they were so opposite. She found Lilly fascinating. Lilly actually cried during *Horrible Bosses* because she found Jennifer Aniston's sexual harassment of Charlie Day so hard to take. Elle laughed gently at how adorable she found this, and even bought Lilly flowers afterward to cheer her up, which brought Lilly more emotion and Elle more bewilderment and fascination.

They were great together, and they were in love. They quickly decided to get an apartment together, neither afraid of the short-for-a-hetero-relationship-but-not-that-short-for-two-women amount of time they had spent together. The apartment they chose was in West L.A. and it was perfect. It had a Victorian feel to it with true crown molding around the ceiling which extended in thin, sparse-ly-placed columns down the walls. The molding was white and the walls a very soft turquoise. With a blend of Lilly's and Elle's styles the apartment looked amazing. Lilly hung some photographs of lilies (how adorably on the nose).Elle offset them with black-and-white stills of different gods of rock she'd purchased at thrift stores over the years, as well as some photos taken on the sets of 90s action movies.

The apartment was a perfect blend of their personalities.

But since the thing that makes someone fall in love is often the very thing that makes them fall out of it, Elle and Lilly began to grow apart. Lilly's robust blend of emotions came along with baggage she had a hard time containing: rage and jealousy. Elle was one to talk an issue through and, once it was done, let it go and move on. Lilly was a dweller. It wouldn't have been so bad if she didn't dwell on things that were not actually problems. She started suspecting Elle was unfaithful when Elle had a particularly big caseload at the center that required her to work long hours. She'd ask Elle about text messages she'd received, making it clear Lilly had gone through her phone. And no matter what she said, Elle couldn't calm her down and couldn't convince Lilly that there was no one else.

Lilly wasn't crazy in the psychopath sense. She was just insecure. And since Elle was her first real relationship, she hadn't yet learned how to work her way through the complicated stuff that came up.

Lilly took it too far the night she came home from yoga to find Jane and Elle talking over wine and whiskey, something that wasn't even a rare event. Some blend of worry and inexperience in Lilly brought her to accuse Elle and Jane of having an affair. Anyone who knew Jane and Elle knew there was *definitely* nothing going on between them. Sure, they were close, but their relationship was clearly more siblings than lovers. It wasn't the final nail in the coffin of the relationship, but it's the nail that made Elle realize there *was* a coffin, and that the relationship was slowly dying.

A few weeks later Elle and Lilly had the final break-up conversation. Though there was love lost with the split, it had to be done. Lilly wasn't ready for this level of commitment and Elle couldn't hand-hold her through it. Lilly needed a few heart breaks under her belt before she'd have the scar tissue necessary to tough it out in the thick of a real, loving relationship.

Nonetheless, the break-up tore Elle up from the inside out. She lost ten pounds that she definitely didn't need to lose, but food disgusted her and she couldn't bring herself to force down more than a few bites at a time. She still went to work, but afterward she'd breakdown. She missed Lilly with a force she wasn't familiar with. She'd never had a break-up before where she didn't genuinely hate the person in the moment, allowing the anger to carry her to emotional safety until she could reevaluate the relationship and realize they simply weren't right for each other.

Lilly had afforded her no such luxury.

Not actually ready to move on from Lilly, Elle was content to go through the motions at work and cry to Jane at night until the pain started to subside. Once it did, Elle found herself in a pattern that didn't include meeting new women and she was ok with that. She went back to men to clear her mind of Lilly. She was attracted to guys too, after all, and they'd be much less likely to remind her of her ex than another woman. Plus, guys were good at one-and-done's, which very much appealed to Elle. Sex with no strings was exactly where she was at. And it was the very thing she was trying to distance herself from in the present.

Elle shook her head to clear the memories. Then her feet moved on their own, seemingly on auto-pilot. She walked straight toward Lilly's table as if on a conveyor belt.

"Hey," Elle offered Lilly, the best olive branch she could muster.

Lilly snapped up at the sound of the familiar voice. Which

she really should have expected, seeing as she was in *Elle's* favorite hang-out. "Elle, um, hi. This is Andrea. My girlfriend."

Ok. She'd wanted Lilly to be happy. She just didn't want to see it. Swallowing the mix of sadness and annoyance that filled her throat, Elle spoke up. "Nice to meet you, Andrea." There, that was mature, right?

"You look good," Lilly added. Elle didn't know what to do with that one. Was Lilly baiting her current girlfriend? Was she really that immature? Still?

Elle cleared her throat. "How'd you two meet?"

Lilly looked at Andrea, stars in her eyes. "I reread *The Knowledge* and I just kind of asked the Universe for her, and there she was."

And there it was. A barely muffled snort sounded from Jane.

Elle wanted good things for her ex but seeing her now, seven years later, still waxing about "the Universe," trying to taunt both her and Andrea, Elle realized something: the good things she wanted for Lilly did not include herself.

After a couple minutes of awkward chit chat, she said goodbye and pulled Jane with her toward their Photo Hunt corner.

"Wow," Elle said.

"How are you? Where are you at right now?" Jane peered at Elle, waiting for her reaction.

Elle replied slowly. "I feel ... done." She paused. "Like, for real."

As she said the words, she knew she meant them. She was finally over Lilly.

Jane actually jumped out of her seat and yelled, "Yes!" as she hugged her best friend. "Fuck yeah, girl," she said to Elle. They clinked glasses, downed their shots, and took on Photo Hunt with renewed excitement.

While Christine got ready for work, Paul came up behind her. "Hey," he said, as she brushed her hair. "I made reservations tonight for a family dinner at Carmine's for seven-thirty."

Well, that was unexpected.

"I know I've been gone a lot lately. I'd like to start making that up to you."

Christine was near speechless. "That…sounds great," she sputtered.

"You look nice, by the way," Paul added as he headed downstairs. It wasn't necessarily a comment on her gym-related weight loss, but it was a start! Maybe, just maybe…things would work out. She shook away a flicker of guilt that invaded her stomach. What happened with Frankie was over. She was focusing on her family, and finally Paul was too.

At work that day she actively avoided Frankie and he seemed to take the hint. After an initial interaction where she gave him a close-lipped, business smile he steered clear of her office. At five sharp, she left the office and headed to her kids' after school care. Her bouncing children were visibly excited for dinner with Daddy, since they hadn't eaten with Paul in a long time . Once home, Chris popped in a movie for the kids to watch while she showered. Then she helped them pick out outfits for their "fancy night" as Cameron called it.

Chris put on a sleek but family-friendly black dress and applied make-up carefully. Her head was all over the place, but that didn't mean her looks had to be. Paul had planned to meet them at the restaurant, so at seven the crew piled into the mini-van and set out on their adventure.

Christine ordered a glass of chardonnay for herself and diet coke for the kids while they waited for Paul. And waited.

And waited.

Thirty minutes and five "are you *sure* I can't get you guys anything?" questions from the server later, Chris got a text.

Hi hon. Sorry, running late. Be @ 8.

Ugh. He couldn't even make it on time to the family night *he* had set up. Reactively, Chris checked to see if Frankie had texted and when she saw he had not, fronts of relief and disappointment collided inside of her. *Focus on your children,* she scolded herself.

She ordered appetizers to tide the kids over until Paul arrived. Hungry kids got cranky fast and she wanted them to enjoy this night. The kids' menu had mini pizzas as a starter, which she knew would go over well with her crew.

Eight came and went and at eight-fifteen Chris checked her phone again.

Not going to make it. Tell the kids I'm so sorry, Paul texted.

Christine held back the tears welling up behind her eyes. She didn't care that much for herself. Hell, she had gotten used to Paul's absence. The kids, however, still needed their father. She hated the looks on their faces when she had to say that Daddy wasn't coming. She felt like a single parent whose kids were waiting by the door, excited for Daddy to take them for the weekend, only she knew Daddy wasn't coming.

"Guys, bad news. Daddy can't make it. He's working really hard and he loves you a lot and is sorry."

Her babies' faces dropped. "Daddy's always gone," Lucy stated accurately.

"I'm sorry. I know it sucks. But we can still have fun!" She mustered as much enthusiasm as she could and gave her kids a fun, "fancy night." They spoke in British accents, drank their beverages with pinkies out, and, after dinner, ordered cream puffs for dessert.

At home that evening, after the kids had been tucked in, Paul walked in the door. Christine, tired of bottling her emotions, let him have it.

"What the fuck is going on with you lately? You're never home and your kids miss you. You really hurt them tonight."

"Chris, I know and I'm sorry. I know I'm disappointing you."

"No. Enough with the apologies. I'm sick of them," Chris said through gritted teeth.

"I understand that. But I don't know what to do. My job, they need me."

"No, your children need you, Paul," she spewed with venom.

Paul winced. "You're right. I know that. But Christine, I'm prepping for a mediation. Things are crazy right now."

"What's crazy is that you're a ghost around here."

"I'm trying, I just--" Paul began.

"How? *How* are you trying? Because I just spoke to your children in a British accent all night so they could forget the fact that *you weren't there.*"

Christine recognized the defeated look in Paul's eye and she didn't care. No, she was *happy* about it.

"And I know what you're really doing Paul. I've found hints around the house. I see how that woman Angela looks at you."

Paul looked at his wife.

"You're having an affair." There! She had said it!

"Christine, please. It's just work." Paul, turning to walk upstairs added over his shoulder, "I'm no more having an affair than you are."

Oh God. Punched in the gut. The image and taste of Frankie's kiss filled her mouth. She wiped it away, recommitting to the idea that it would *never* happen again.

The next morning was Saturday. Paul had mentioned he'd be popping into the office early, so Chris assumed he'd be gone all day. But by noon, he was back home and ready to hang out with his family. Her kids jumped for joy when Daddy walked in the door. His smile was just as big as theirs.

Ok, perhaps things could get back on track. Maybe last night's conversation had made an impact and they'd be ok after all.

Cam had been asking to go to the zoo recently, so they decided to go. Paul and Chris packed a picnic and hauled the herd to see wild animals and eat some lunch. Wanting to clear the tension without cueing in the kids, Chris simply asked her husband, "Are we ok?"

"I am. Are you?" he replied.

"I think so."

With that, the fight was over. Or at least on pause. And for now, Chris was ok with that.

The zoo was an absolute blast. Lucy got to pet a goat and Cameron made faces at an orangutan who made some back. That night the family ate dinner together and the kids filled Paul in on the details of their fancy dinner the night before. Whew! Chris had pulled it off; they'd had fun!

After dinner they played a board game and they wrapped up the evening with everyone saying what their favorite part of the day had been.

"I liked the animals," Lucy offered. "And being with Daddy." Christine smiled.

Cameron's turn. "I liked the orangutan and being with my family." Adorable.

Christine spoke up. "Well, I enjoyed every minute of being with all of you."

"So did I," Paul added, smiling at his wife.

After the kids went to bed, Christine cleaned up a bit while Paul watched TV. He offered to help but she was happy to have alone time to reflect on the day. It had truly been a good one. She wrapped up the chores and joined Paul in the living room. After a bit, he piped up.

"Hey. I had a great time with you and the kids today," Paul said sincerely.

"I did too," Chris said as she smiled at her husband.

"It was nice spending the entire day together, as a family," Paul added.

"Yeah, we could...we *should*...do it more often. If you want."

"I do!" he added emphatically. "I just, you know. We will."

Neither knew what to say, and neither wanted to continue the conversation from last night. Deciding they should leave the day as a good memory, Christine said she was tired and suggested they call it a night.

With that they went upstairs for a passionless night of sleep in the same bed.

Before falling asleep, Chris found herself gently crying, saddened by how rare it was to have a nice day with her husband lately. She mourned the loss of the excitement in life she used to feel with him. Of course, life wasn't a continuous stream of new adventures, and when she chose to, she could see her relationship with her children as a new adventure every day.

But as she thought about her relationship with her husband, she realized they felt more like friends than partners and even their friendship felt tired. Did all couples go through this? Chris wasn't sure, and she wasn't convinced she cared. She knew how she wanted her own relationship to feel and this wasn't it.

Of course, she had fouled hard recently, but it had been Paul who'd been spending so much time away from the family. He did work hard, but what—besides Angela—could be such a draw to be away from home? For a person to spend so much time away, they must be avoiding something.

Or someone.

Chris had a sudden flash of insight. Was *she* the reason for his absence? Had he picked up on her unhappiness and dissatisfaction? She and Paul had not been communicating. How was it that after so many years of marriage she didn't know if he was fucking someone else? How did he not know that she felt like shit about herself and had borderline cheated on him? Though this seemed like new territory for the seasoned couple, clearly they had been walking down this path for quite some time. People didn't just land here out of the blue.

Paul was home for a bit on Sunday, though not as much as Christine had hoped. And come Monday, things were back to the new normal. Christine worked and raised her kids while her husband "worked." She didn't feel Paul come in that night, but when she woke in the morning there was evidence of his having been there. Specifically, he had left a note.

I'm sorry I missed you last night. I'm trying, I really am but it's hard. I promise I'll be home tonight—early!—so we can finish talking it out. I love you.

This brought a tear to Chris's eye. Ok, he was sorry. And genuinely so. And now he was ready to talk about it. In depth. This was a very good step.

As Chris was about to get up, her kids came barreling into her room and snuggled in bed with her.

"We love you Mommy," Lucy said.

"Yeah," Cam agreed.

God, children were so pure.

"I love you both more than you'll ever know," Chris said with more force than she'd intended. She kissed her children, enjoyed a few minutes of snuggle time and then corralled them toward the bathroom to start getting ready for school.

CHAPTER TWELVE

Once the weekend came, it was time for Jane to go to camp. Excited enough about her new lead, she drove like a maniac nearly causing three minor collisions along the way. Bombarded by a barrage of honking horns and middle fingers, she finally arrived in front of Kreative Kids. "Ugh," she muttered aloud as she realized it was one of those places that misspelled their names to be cute (sorry, "kute").

She walked into the K.K. and was immediately met with the welcoming smell of finger paints and acrylics. Ahhh. As she took in the figure behind the counter, Stevie Nicks singing "Gypsy" immediately filled in her head. The White Witch looked to be in her mid-50s which was a good sign. She could have worked here when Ridgeley was a camper!

"Can I help you?" Stevie asked in a voice much higher than her doppelganger's gravelly vocals.

"Hi, yeah, I'm hoping to talk to someone who has worked here for a long time. Would that be you?"

"Sorry, I'm actually new. Did you just think I'd worked here for a long time since I'm older?"

"Um..."

"It's ok dear, it happens all the time. I'm a student at USC. Most of the teachers here are college students."

"Oh, ok."

"You sound surprised. Are you surprised I'm a college student because I'm older?"

What the fuck? The Stevie obviously had a complex. "I in no way indicated surprise," Jane retorted. "Is there anyone here who has worked here longer than you? Or like, anyone else here at all?"

"Let me get my manager." Stevie walked away, shaking her head.

As Jane waited, she meandered around the open space a bit. Kids were working on various art projects. She saw a somewhat frustrated little girl who was trying to translate a figurine of a puppy to paper with colored pencils. Sensing that the girl was unhappy with her work, Jane walked over. "Cool picture," Jane offered.

"No it's not," the Addison replied. "I can't get the face right."

Jane glanced at her paper. She was right. This Addy had been trying to capture the dog's face before nailing the outline of the head. Rookie mistake, which made sense since the kid was like eight years old. "Know what? It'll be easier if you do the outline of the head first like this." Jane drew the outline on a sheet of scratch paper. "Once you have the outline, you can see where the features can be dropped in."

Jane sketched it out and the Addison was impressed. "Cool. Thanks!" Jane smiled. She might have just taught a child something useful about art. Addy tried it out and her work was immediately more accurate.

"Can I help you?" a woman asked, a bit louder than necessary. "Can you come back over here, and not by the kids? We can't just have random adults wandering around."

Oh, shit. Of course. "Sorry," Jane said. "I'm not molest-y, I promise." As if that made it better.

"How can I help you?" The woman looked to be about Jane's age, with short punky brown hair wrapped in a head-band style bandanna; a total Meg.

"I need to find this woman. She used to come to this camp as a child," Jane explained. She showed the picture of Ridgeley to the woman, who took it in with intent.

"See, the problem is this is a summer camp for kids. You're showing me a drawing of a grown adult. Also, almost all of our employees are college kids so there's a lot of turn-over."

"Not all kids! Some of us are older," Stevie called out from the back room. Jesus. The Meg rolled her eyes. "Anyway, most are college students here for the summer. I'm the only full-timer, and I started 2 years ago. I'm afraid I can't help."

No! This couldn't be where her search ended. Then Jane had an idea. "Records! You must have records of who the teachers were in the past. I need to know who taught here during summers in the early 90s!"

Meg looked at her like she was a crazy person. Which perhaps she was, but Jane had no time to worry about that

"Yeah, this is a summer camp, not a University. We don't still have all of our records from the early 90s."

"What about electronically? Someone must have scanned them in at some point."

Meg looked skeptical. "I feel like you watch a lot of CSI. Despite popular belief, not all things get scanned in to a database. This being a non-profit art camp, nobody has ever been hired to scan records of things that don't matter at all from 30 years ago."

"Fuck," Jane said. Meg looked over toward the kids. "Sorry," Jane apologized. She wasn't giving up. "There must be something. Owners? Who are the owners? Maybe I can talk to them!"

Meg's facial expression definitely conveyed thoughts of Jane having a serious diagnosis. "What's your deal?" she asked.

Jane took a deep breath, exhaled, and went there. She told Meg everything about her mission. As she spoke, Meg's facial expression softened slightly.

"Look. Your plan sounds ridiculous, and like it will never give you what you're truly looking for, but I get it. Kind of." Oh, thank God. "I can't give out the owners' personal info, because that's crazy. But I can tell you how to find them. Also, Google is a thing."

"Touché," Jane responded.

Meg continued. "There's an event downtown L.A. every Wednesday night. I've never been but I know it's a thing where local artists get together to display their work and occasionally sell it. Anyway, the owners of Kreative Kids run it. Good luck."

"Thank you, Meg!"

Meg started. "Wait, how did you know my name?" Holy shit. Her name really was Meg.

"I didn't," Jane spat out as she rushed out the door. Success! She had helped a young girl with her art and picked up another clue that could lead her one step closer to Ridgeley!

* * *

That evening, Chris sat fidgeting on her couch, nervously waiting for Paul to get home. After reading his note she'd been a mess all day, vacillating between hope and fear over the outcome of their conversation. Was he really cheating on her? Could she admit she'd contemplated the same?

It was amazing she'd managed to do any work today, particularly since she'd been working from home. On the plus side, that meant she hadn't had any run-ins with Frankie. She still felt a pulse in her panties every time she thought about Frankie's stupid sideways smile, the smell of him, the bulge of his muscles under his shirt. *God,* he was sexy.

No, stop it. She had a husband to reconcile with. She needed to put Frankie out of her mind. Thank God they'd only flirted and kissed once. It was nothing irredeemable. Even if she wasn't sure she what she wanted to come from this conversation with Paul, at least she knew that, if they wanted to, they could fix things.

Her phone buzzed. Paul. *I'm so sorry, something came up. Home late.*

That. Was. It!

She began typing. *What are you doing in 30?*

Nothing. Where to? Frankie responded immediately.

Next, she texted Jane. *Can you come over and watch the kids?*
Yep, no problem.

Meet me at the same place as last time, she texted Frankie.

Twenty minutes later, Jane walked through the front door. "Party's here," she shouted to the kids, to which they responded with shrieks and giggles. "Damn, where to?" she asked her sister, eyeing her up and down suspiciously.

"I'll explain later. And thank you!" Chris said as she ran out the door. She knew her low-cut shirt and tight skirt would raise her sister's eyebrow, but that it would not elicit suspicion with her innocent young children. She paid no attention to the speed limit as she raced to the bar. Pulling in the driveway, she spotted Frankie outside and rolled down her window, waving him over. He walked toward her with purpose. She opened her driver's door and pulled him down toward her for a deep, intense kiss that set her on fire. "Get in," she said simply.

Chris drove them to a corner of the parking lot that was relatively empty, shifted into park and ripped off her seatbelt. Diving toward him, her lips attacked her young lover, a very willing recipient. Groping, gasping for air, their tongues practically danced. Frankie's hand slid over her shirt and she moaned inadvertently.

As they continued to feel each other up PG-13 style, they moved to the back seat like a couple of sixteen-year-olds ready to explore the opposite sex for the first time. Christine knew this was high-risk, hooking up like an adolescent in a car in a public parking lot, but at the moment, she didn't care. All she cared about was experiencing as much of Frankie as she possibly could. He wet his fingers, slipping them under her panties and inside of her. She moaned and writhed.

Fuck it, she couldn't resist him anymore.

With her right hand, she pulled Frankie toward her, begging him to go inside. "Are you sure?" he asked. This was it. If she crossed this line, there was no going back. This was cheating plain and simple, but Christine was too far gone in lust to care. A flash of Paul crossed her mind and she shook it away. Looking deep into Frankie's eyes, she answered him. "I'm fucking positive."

With that, he slipped on a condom and slipped inside her. It was everything she had imagined. New cock felt beyond amazing. She moaned in ecstasy, riding him slowly. He grabbed her hair pulling her head back a bit. She responded by snapping to attention, staring deep into his eyes until she finished, and allowed him to follow suit.

As Frankie let out his final groan, her stomach dropped. Oh God, her husband. Her children. What had she just done? Crying, she quickly dismounted him, pulled on her panties and skirt and exited the vehicle. "Christine? Are you ok?" a confused Frankie called after her.

"I have to go. I'm so sorry, Frankie. I shouldn't have done this. I'm sorry," she said through tears. She began to leave, then realized it was her own car. Her head was everywhere. *What had she just done?*

She cried the whole way home, barely able to see the road through her clouded tears, filled with lust and regret. What the fuck had happened to her marriage? Pulling in the driveway, she wiped the tears off her face. She had to get it together; she couldn't let her kids see her like this. Thank God Jane was there.

"Mommy!" her children yelled as she walked in. That felt like a nail to the stomach. Criminals didn't deserve gifts from children. Taking one glimpse at her big sis, Jane re-directed the kids.

"Moms needs some alone time babies. She's gonna go upstairs and I will be right back."

Christine took the gift and went upstairs. Not knowing what the fuck to do with herself, she drew a bath, sat in it, and allowed the tears to flow. A few minutes in, Jane popped in with a glass of chardonnay.

"Looks like you could use this. Let me know when you're ready to talk," she said, then ran back downstairs to hang with Chris's children.

A tear-filled Chris sipped the wine and attempted to wash away her sins.

* * *

Across town, Elle pulled up to a house off Melrose. She immediately spotted three young thirty-something ladies in cocktail dresses and too-high heels bubbling toward the door of the very house she was intent on entering. She looked down, taking in her black tank and tattered jeans. This would be an interesting night if nothing else.

Shaking off her doubts, Elle stuck her boot-clad feet out of her car door and strutted her ass toward Amber-and-company's house party. She was doing it. Outside of the comfort zone, yet again. She had brought along two bottles of wine. Not her drink of choice, but it seemed a safe bet with this crowd.

She had a flask full of whiskey for herself. Elle fully planned to spread her wings, but her wings might need a little lubrication.

As she opened the door, she heard a high-pitched, "Hiiiii!" It was Amber. Elle smiled despite herself. She gave Amber a hug, which in and of itself was out of character, and allowed the brunette Barbie to tour her around the party and introduce her to other guests. She smiled as she took in all of the ladies in short little dress-es, looking girly and perfect, and the bro-dogs with man-buns. Jane would've had a field day here. Elle settled in, leaning against the back of the couch. Would she have anything in common with Amber's guests? She wasn't sure, but she's was up for finding out.

A guy approached her. He was hot, but in a douchey way which wasn't Elle's style. "Hey. Rad jacket," he said. "Where'd you get that?"

As Elle looked around, she realized her effortless fashion was still accidentally in style. Maybe she wasn't so out of place here after all.

She hung with the guy whose name was Anthony (Jane would have called him "Dax," or something similar) for a good twenty minutes. He wasn't hitting on her at all. In fact, he was just a cool guy looking to have a conversation.

After a bit, Amber circled back around. "How's it going so far?" she asked Elle.

"Good. Your friends are cool."

"They are. I'm glad you came," Amber said sincerely.

They got into a long-ish conversation in which Elle revealed more of herself than she had anticipated. She talked about her dating life, the fact that she was bisexual and even mentioned Lilly. Then, Amber got momentarily lame. She did the typical straight girl thing of pitching her only lesbian friend to Elle. "I feel like you'd like her."

Because all women who like women are into each other. She wanted to nip this one in the bud. "Dude. I doubt it."

Amber replied, "I mean, FYI I don't just think all lesbians or bisexual women are into each other." Amber continued. "She's like a hippie chick; very Joni Mitchell. I feel like you'd be into that. I don't know why. She'll be here in a bit so you can judge for yourself."

Maybe Amber was the exception to the rule. This girl actually did sound up Elle's alley. "We'll see," Elle hedged.

They continued chatting until hostessing duties pulled Amber away. Elle chilled for a bit longer, and just as she was about to head out, someone headed in. She was cute, in her flowy skirt and fairy necklace. Hippie Joni Mitchell indeed; this was obviously the woman Amber had been talking about. She waited as Joni made her rounds, not wanting to jump in too eagerly. Once Joni was settled, never the one to be shy, Elle approached.

"I dig your necklace," she opened.

"Why thank you. I like your jacket. Very Linda Hamilton." Whoa. An immediate 90s action reference. This bode well.

"I'm Elle."

"Daria. Nice to meet you."

Elle sat down.

"So, what's your story?" Daria asked. Elle cracked a smile. It was a broad question but she dove in.

"Well, I'm a social worker—I work at the LGBTQ center—and I met Amber the other night while I was out just exploring the city."

"Oh, you're a tourist," Daria assumed.

"No, I'm from here. I just try to find different ways to see the city, you know?"

"Not really, but I'm intrigued," Daria responded.

"I mean, I'll pick a neighborhood and go in somewhere I've never been. Like the other night I checked out a random hole-in-the wall in Boyle Heights. It had amazing Mexican food. And it reminds me that no matter how long I've lived here, there's always something new to see."

"Very cool."

"Your turn," Elle passed the conversation back.

"I work in PR but I make jewelry on the side for fun. Like this necklace, for example. And I know Amber because she's bought some from me."

"Nice."

As the women started talking, Elle felt comfort take over. Talking to Daria was easy. With Lilly now fully in her past, maybe she *was* actually ready to connect with a woman. As Daria spoke, Elle saw a motion out of the corner of her eye. Looking left, she saw Amber mouthing the most obvious "I told you so" possible, and she couldn't help but laugh.

"What?" Daria asked.

"Amber. She told me about you before you got here. She thought we'd hit it off."

"Hmm. I think she might be on to something," Daria responded. And with that, Elle was officially open to getting to know Daria.

CHAPTER THIRTEEN

Jane filled her week with work, couch, and wine. Sunday night, she joined Chris and the kids at her parents' house for family dinner with grandma. On the ride home, Lucy asked to stop for ice-cream, despite having just finished a feast. When Christine said no, Lucy responded, "I know. I can't get everything I want, just some of it." Jane was shocked. That was the lesson from her book!

Christine looked at her sister. "I re-read it you know. I stand by the fact that it's crazy but you did have some valid points. I actually pulled some usable content from it."

Monday and Tuesday included messages and phone calls with Dave and finally Wednesday arrived, bringing with it the event aptly named "Downtown Art." Jane had googled the crap out of it. She now knew the names of the people she was looking for: Al and Mara Olson. Though they ran the event, Jane figured they'd be relatively easy to access since this wasn't exactly The Getty, and they weren't exactly Robert Mapplethorpe and Patty Smith.

To prove to herself what a good world citizen she was, and because parking was always a pain downtown, Jane took the train to the event. It was relatively close to Seventh and Metro, one of the stops on her line. She could use the walk between the station and the art show to get her head in the zone.

She had half considered inviting Elle to come with her tonight, but at the last second she chickened out. Though the odds were against it, what if Ridgeley was there? What if she had an actual run-in with her former nemesis-who-was-never-actually-her-nemesis? Jane didn't know what she'd do, but she knew she wouldn't want anyone to see her reaction.

Rocking a standard blue t-shirt and jeans, she exited the train station downtown and took a left to head toward the event. After a few short blocks, she was there. It was a fairly small affair; she wasn't surprised she hadn't heard of it before. For one, she had kept her ear far away from the art scene and for two, there were only about ten booths. There was something comforting in the size of the event. It seemed neighborly in a way that Jane liked instead of hated. Artists here probably actually talked to each other and shared tips rather than competing like they did at bigger events.

She stopped at the first booth, checking out the table of dull silver twisted metal sculptures. Some of them were cool as fuck. One was a single piece of metal bent into the shape of a tornado. Another had spears of silver stabbing inward to a center that, in the densest meeting of the metals, formed the shape of a human heart. Damn.

"Hey, I'm Brandon," said the artist. Wow. She hadn't even been given time to make up a name for him.

"Jane," she responded. "Your shit is amazing," she added.

Brandon thanked her and began describing his pieces and his process to her. He asked her about herself. "Are you an artist, Miss Jane?"

"Yes. I mean no. Yes. I am, but I've been on a hiatus for like … fifteen years. Or so."

Brandon raised his eyebrows in amusement. "No time like the present to get back in. You should talk to the organizers, Al and Mara."

This would be easier than she thought. Brandon told her what booth to find them in and Jane, though intending to bee-line toward them, sort of bumbled her way there taking in the wonderful art around her. She dug this vibe, but immediately regretted thinking the words "dug" and "vibe."

She picked up parts of conversations between the artists and the pedestrians checking out their wares. Though she heard some cringe-worthy buzz words like "conviviality" and "idiosyncratic," the artists that uttered them seemed truly genuine instead of the run-of-the-mill pretentious museum critics who spoke similarly. There was definitely a feel of realness to the people gathered here. They loved art because they loved creating, not because they loved speaking nonsense.

She chatted with a couple other people on her way to find her marks. Every one of them invited her to come back or to share a booth with them in the future. Evidently, booths at this event were free as long as you were invited to work in one. This was more a community of like-minded people who wanted to share their work than anything else. While Jane obviously struggled with the idea of aligning herself with anything that could be described as a commune, she had a feeling that this might be a good fit for her. That is, if she decided to paint again. Maybe.

Finally, after fully taking in the scene, she approached the booth that housed Al and Mara, the event coordinators and potential Ridgeley acquaintances. Al's appearance was exactly as Jane had predicted. He had an ex-rock-n-roll vibe, with a leathery face that had seen a lot of drugs. Mara was a bit different. She gave off the air of a woman who had seen things, but then settled into the role of cookie-baking grandma. It was as if Jerry Garcia's Mountain Girl had moved to Wisconsin and volunteered at a library.

Like the others Jane had talked to, they were friendly and inviting. Jane introduced herself, and complemented the atmosphere they had created despite the surroundings of downtown L.A. They explained that they cared about showing art in communities that didn't always have the opportunity to see it. Despite the many art museums downtown, the socio-economic divide prevented many of the local residents from seeing and interacting with quality art. Though the art at this event was for sale and sales were made, the over-arching intent of it—to showcase something beautiful—was a bit more altruistic.

Jane cut to the chase. "I'm looking for an old friend of mine. Her name is Ridgeley and I think she used to attend your camp." Jane filled them in on Ridgeley's history: that she had been a student at their art camp back in the 90s.

"Well, that's when our granddaughter was at the camp."

"Oh my God, maybe your granddaughter is who I'm looking for!"

Mara walked away to dig through her purse. Praying her hunch was correct, Jane waited for Mara to return with a photograph of the girl.

Jane started. "Wait, your granddaughter is black?" Oops. "I mean..."

"It's ok, we get that a lot. Our son was adopted."

Apparently, they'd been ahead of their time, adopting kids to create an interracial family before it was cool. Good for them, but bad for her. This girl was categorically not Ridgeley.

Jane pulled out her sketch of Ridgeley, but as she had guessed, they were not able to recognize an adult version of her. Then, lightning struck. "Do you have a pencil and a piece of paper?" Jane asked.

"Of course," Al replied, pulling one from his vest.

Jane quickly drew Ridgeley's signature, the stylistic outline of a cat.

"Does this look familiar? Ridgeley signed all of her work like this in college."

Al took a look and poked Mara. "Hey Mar, take a look at this. Didn't Hannah used to always draw a cat like this?"

Mara moved her glasses down the bridge of her nose to get a better look. She zeroed in on the picture. "Hannah didn't draw this. Her *friend* did."

Game back on! Jane held her breath.

"What friend?" Al asked.

Mara, looking disappointed in her husband's memory, filled in his gaps. "You know exactly who. Geraldine."

"My God, you're right," Al added. "They used to pretend they were that awful band all the time and dance around the living room. That pop group, Bang or something."

Jane jumped in. "You mean Wham!? Was it Wham!?"

Mara looked at her. "Yes! That was it! They used to always sing that Jitterbug song."

"Oh yeah!" Al mused. "Hannah was always the lead singer, and Geraldine was the other one."

"Hannah was George Michael and her friend was … Andrew Ridgeley," Jane filled in.

"That was it. God, they were obsessed. Can't believe I didn't remember that."

Ridgeley.

George Michael and Andrew *Ridgeley*.

Holy fuck, Ridgeley was a nickname referencing the other guy from Wham! and Ridgeley's real name was *Geraldine?* No wonder she went with a nickname.

Jane couldn't believe it. Was she finally going to find Ridgeley and get the painting back?

"Do you know where Geraldine is?"

Mara looked conflicted. "We haven't spoken with her in probably 30 years. But she was a very private person. I don't feel like we can tell you much more."

Jane pivoted. "Can I talk to Hannah? Maybe she'll be willing to spill!"

Mara and Al looked sullen. "I'm sorry darling, Hannah's passed."

Oh, shit! "I'm so sorry." Jane guilelessly pushed on. "What about her father? Maybe he'll know something?"

"Darling, it was a car accident. He's passed as well."

"How convenient," Jane muttered, filter-less.

"Pardon me?" Mara questioned.

181

Shit! "Sorry for your loss!" But Jane was on the train and it wasn't slowing down. She kept moving forward. "What about your son's widow? Can you call her? I need to find this girl."

Al cleared his throat and responded far too empathetically. "Miss, this tragedy changed our family. We haven't spoken to her in years. So, no. We will not call our late son's widow after years of silence to ask if she remembers someone we just told you is very private and may not want to be found."

Jane had officially gone too far. She apologized profusely for her lack of tact and her singular focus. She had blown this interaction and made a mental note to fix it later.

After saying goodbye to the Olsons, Jane took a pamphlet for the event that included a calendar of upcoming dates. Armed with her new intel on Ridgeley, she forged onward toward the end of her mission.

When she got home, she got to work. Jane now had a new piece of information to help her find … Geraldine. No, she had two. She immediately googled "Wham! fan club + Geraldine." Nothing. She wasn't surprised. When Jane and Ridgeley (she just *couldn't* call her Geraldine) were kids, the Internet wasn't a thing. Ridgeley likely didn't continue her Wham! obsession into adulthood, because who would do that?

The next search was "Geraldine + art." Optimistic, Jane hit search and held her breath. She scrolled through the articles that had populated. Link by link, she lost hope. She entered as many other search words as she could find. No dice.

Then she had an idea. She quickly googled Hannah Olson obituary. Boom. She now had the adult face of Hannah Olson, Al and Mara's late granddaughter. The article said that when she passed, she had been living in New York. From a bit of googling, Jane learned that family members didn't usually shut down their deceased love ones' Facebook pages.

That said, finding a Hannah Olson in New York on Facebook could prove difficult. It was a fairly common name in a populated place, but she had a photograph and plenty of time.

A half hour and two glasses of wine in, she struck gold. There she was, Hannah Olson (RIP). Jane clicked on her face and as her page populated, sadness hit. Hannah's page was filled with tearful messages from friends and family telling her how much they missed her. God, this was a real human being who had passed and Jane had spoken to her grandparents as though she were a piece of a puzzle. Disgusting. Next plan of action would be to revisit Al and Mara with a bigger apology and something to back it up.

Jane continued scrolling as she thought through her plan of recompense. She froze. There was a link to the video for "I'm Your Man" by Wham! posted by someone named Geraldine Braunger.

Instead of a selfie for a profile picture, there was a drawing of a very familiar cat outline.

She had found Ridgeley.

"Holy fuck I found her!" she practically yelled. She immediately texted Chris. Grandma was going to be so surprised. But there was someone else she wanted to tell. Picking up the phone, she called Dave.

"Janey!" he answered.

As he did, tears welled up in Jane's eyes. Hearing her friend's voice, paired with finally achieving her goal of finding Ridgeley hit her beautifully. "Dave. I found her."

Dave paused. Oh, God, what was he going to say? "Jane. I'm *so fucking happy for you!*"

"I couldn't have done it without you," she began. "I mean, maybe I could have. But I'm really happy I didn't have to."

"Me too," he added simply.

"Thank you so much. I mean really. For everything." She wiped tears of gratitude from her eyes. Thinking back on college, things had really come full circle. And this time around, she was doing it right. No more blaming others for her own failures. She'd finally grown up.

But enough reminiscing on personal growth. She had work to do! Hanging up with Dave, she got back to it.

When she clicked on the name Geraldine Braunger in Facebook, she wasn't surprised to see the account was set to private. Because of course it was. She didn't care. She now had a full name, and an uncommon one at that.

She hit up Google and scrolled through the results, past pages for Andrew Lehman, Tiana, Pilar Montenegro and other artists with styles similar to Ridgeley's. There was apparently a NYC makeup artist named Geraldine Braunger but she was in her fifties. A CFO Geraldine Braunger whose mugshot showed she was definitely NOT Ridgeley. A high school volleyball-playing Geraldine Braunger. What else could she add to her search? The only thing she knew, the only thing she came up with was that fucking picture of the cat. She added "cat" to her search terms and *voilá*. Braunger's Babies veterinary clinic outside of Davis, California. Needless to say, the place had no website because that would be too easy. However, the side of her search window populated with a picture and some contact information. Holy shit. The practice's logo was Ridgeley's famous cat picture. And there was a phone number.

It was way too late now to call, as the business was certainly closed, so Jane did the next best thing and called Elle.

"Oh my God, well done!" Elle responded as Jane yelled her success at her.

Jane filled her in over the next twenty minutes. As the conversation wound to an end, Elle piped up. "By the way, we're going out tomorrow night and you're gonna hate it. Later!" With that, she hung up.

The next morning, Jane was up at 8:00am. Without thinking, she pulled up the number for Braunger's Babies and dialed. A receptionist answered and Jane choked. "Is Ridge…is…is this the office of Geraldine Braunger?"

Without skipping a beat, the receptionist replied, "Yes, it is. How can I help you?"

"Um...Wait, are you open on weekends?" she managed.

"We are," the receptionist replied.

Jane hung up.

Smooth. She didn't even care. She had done it. She had fucking found Ridgeley. And she was a fucking veterinarian? That's what the cats were all about, literal cats? These were questions for Ridgeley, who she could now speak to. She could complete her journey, get her painting back, and make Grandma happy!

She knew she couldn't initiate the long-overdue conversation with Ridgeley over the phone. Who would react well to that? "Hi, we met in college, and I accused you of stealing my life. Wanna talk?" Instead she vowed to take a road trip on Saturday. Well, maybe not this Saturday. She had to mentally prep. But the next Saturday for sure!

With more excitement than she could bury inside herself,

Jane threw on her running clothes and sprinted outside. This time she wasn't running from anything. She was running toward herself. "Barf," she said out loud. Then she ran her ass off and got ready for work.

* * *

That night, Elle rolled up to Jane's at 9pm. They were leaving the house and they weren't going to KC's. Elle was shocked Jane didn't even fight back when she told her they'd be going to a bar in Hollywood that quote "did not allow rubber soled shoes." Damn, this Ridgeley thing really had her best friend in a new headspace. What Jane didn't know was that Daria would be there. Elle was interested in her, but she didn't want to tip her hat to Jane. She wanted her friend's honest opinion (as if she'd ever offer something different). But Elle also wanted Jane to meet Amber. Her social circle was actually starting to expand. It was amazing. Jane wasn't the only one accomplishing her goal!

"So, is this one of your places you found in your wanderings through L.A.?" Jane asked.

"No, actually. We're going to meet a new friend of mine. I've been meeting new people. She's just a friend—totally straight. Her name is Amber."

Jane scowled. "*Amber?* And we're going to *Hollywood?*"

There it was. "Yes," Elle headed her off at the pass. "And she's bringing some friends that I kind of know. So behave."

Elle and Jane walked into the bar and Jane immediately about-faced and walked out. Having anticipated this very move, Elle was prepared to follow. She grabbed Jane's arm, gave her a "be better" look, and pulled her back in. Amber waved at Elle from the bar.

"Hiiii," the Barbie squealed as she hugged Elle. "Amber, this is Jane," Elle said. Amber hugged Jane, who was a bit less enthusiastic than Elle. "Oh, chill out honey. My girliness won't rub off on you." Elle laughed at Amber; she nailed Jane perfectly. This would be an interesting experiment of new and old worlds colliding.

Jane fired back. "So Amber, what kind of acting do you do?"

Not missing a beat but noticing the dig, Amber replied, "Well, I've done a few commercials, which I can sense you'd think is lame, but I made a shitload of money so who's the joke on?" Elle laughed. Damn, Amber! She went on, "Jane, how much time did you spend today wallowing in self-pity that you created?"

Touché. "Only about an hour," Jane bragged.

Elle was living for this. Jane and Amber were having fun with each other, in a bitchy kind of way.

"Hey Amber," Jane went on, "how was your pumpkin spiced latte today?"

Amber replied, "Oh, come on, you know you love those."

Jane and Elle looked at each other. "Um, no. I've never had one, because obviously," Jane replied, borderline offended.

Amber froze. "Shut the fuck up." She looked between Jane and Elle. "I mean, I get the joke, but seriously? They're fucking delicious." Elle and Jane stared back blankly. "No, Uh-uh." Amber got up and ran out.

"Oh, shit," Jane said apologetically to Elle.

"She'll be back," Elle replied. After all, they were meeting other people here. In fact, where was Daria? Just then, returning from the bathroom, Daria appeared in her periphery, making a smile crack across Elle's face.

"Hey you," Daria said easily, squeezing Elle's shoulder.

"Good to see you," Elle said kissing her on the cheek. "This is Jane. Jane, meet Daria."Elle checked Jane's face and immediately recognized that she got it.

"Nice to meet you," Jane said, "and you are *such* a Daria," she added warmly, taking in Daria's flowy hippie dress. Elle could sense her friend's approval of her potential love interest.

A few minutes later, Amber ran back in, PSL in hand. "Ok. Now seriously, don't be too judge-y to give this a fair shot."

Elle reached for the cup but Jane beat her to it. As Jane took a slow swig, her mouth fell open. "FUCK!" she yelled. "That's fucking delicious." Elle went next. "Huh. Not bad." More than anything, she was impressed by her new friend. She wasn't intimidated by any of Jane's bullshit. She was unapologetically Pumpkin Spiced Amber.

As the night went on, Elle and Daria broke off from the group to hang out on their own. They sank into a comfortable lounge chair, quite close to each other.

"Hey, tell me more about your job at the center," Daria started.

Elle smiled, glad Daria had remembered. "I mostly do one-on-one counseling with teens. But I also run some social activities, just to give them something to do. Especially the ones who have nowhere else to go."

"Do you ever invite guests? I mean, maybe I could do like a jewelry-making thing."

This was a good sign. "Yeah, that'd be awesome."

The women continued to get to know each other, and after a couple more drinks, Elle made a move. Softly touching the side of Daria's face to gauge her reaction, noticing her leaning in, Elle kissed her on the lips. She heard a notable "yesssss" from Jane across the bar and smiled.

They kissed sensually and sweetly. God, Elle had missed women. And this particular one was very intriguing.

Before the evening closed, she and Daria planned a dinner date and Elle agreed to call her the next day.

* * *

Christine pushed her way through work, avoiding contact with everyone she could. She was in a tornado of her own making; a giant man-made storm she couldn't escape. And it didn't help that Paul was still MIA, likely fucking Angela.

She shook her head. It wasn't even definite he was having an affair. The only definite was that *she* had.

After work, she made dinner for her children and played with them until bed time. Thank God they hadn't noticed anything was up with her. She could only hate herself more if she harmed their innocence. Sitting on the couch alone, watching TV, the tears began to fall again. And she could take no more. She picked up her phone. *We need to talk*, she texted.

Immediately, her sister responded. *Be there in 20.*

Jane set the kids up with a movie as Christine sat a frazzled mess in the kitchen. Pouring each a glass of white, Jane held her big sister lovingly as she listened to Christine bare her sins.

"What are you going to do?" Jane asked.

"I don't know. I honestly think Paul is cheating too."

"I'm not convinced," Jane said, "but you guys really need to talk. Badly."

"What do I even say?" Chris asked. "They say never tell someone you've cheated because it only relieves your own conscience."

"I mean, usually. Unless it would do more than relieve your own conscience."

"What do you mean?" Chris asked.

"If you think that knowing you cheated would make Paul want to leave you, you should tell him. It's only fair he be given the opportunity to leave a marriage he wants to leave. You should probably only hold the secret if you think it would hurt him, but not change his decision to stay. You know your husband. What would he want? What would make him happy?"

Chris chewed on this. Her sister was right. She hadn't thought through the fact that Paul might want to leave her, and this sent shivers of pain down her spine.

"It might help to think about what you'd do if he told you he slept with someone else. Would you leave?"

She didn't know what Paul would do with her info about Frankie, or if he was sleeping with Angela. Yet, for the first time in a long time, she knew what she wanted and that was to stay with her husband.

Jane stayed with her sister until Chris fell asleep. Over the next few days, she checked in with Jane regularly. Christine hadn't yet talked to Paul but was steering clear of Frankie. God, what had she done and how was she going to fix it? The only thing she knew for sure is that she needed to talk to her husband.

CHAPTER FOURTEEN

Two weeks later, Elle woke up at her usual time of 6:30am. At least she didn't need to waste money on an alarm clock. Today, per usual, her circadian rhythm served her well since she had a doctor's appointment at 7:30. Normally, Jane would have been the first and only person she'd tell about this kind of procedure, but Elle was too afraid she'd chicken out so she stayed silent. She'd tell Jane after it was over.

As she walked into the clinic, she took in the patients around her. All women with long flowing hair, most with salt-and-pepper-haired husbands who held their hands in support. Oh, boy. She walked to the receptionist and gave her name. "I'm Elle Campton. I'm here to get my eggs frozen."

She'd been telling Jane for weeks she had a weird skin infection, citing antibiotics as the reason she hadn't been drinking. She couldn't bear the look of excitement on her friend's face if she told her what she was actually doing, and then bailed. God, why was getting older so hard? She wasn't even old, but the biological clock was real and science like this scared the shit out of her. Things were promising with Daria. She checked all of Elle's boxes and more, but things were still new and Elle didn't want to push it. Though it had taken her a while to get on board, she had to admit she did like the idea that she was keeping options open and, in a way, freezing time.

The nurse explained to her that the hormones she'd been taking were designed to produce follicles and each follicle had the chance of producing a healthy egg for harvesting. Ideally, there would be at least twenty eggs to harvest, as only half statistically survive. Ten was the ultimate number of freezable eggs they were aiming at. Elle had followed all of the instructions up until now. All she could do was hope her lady parts had done their job and produced what was required.

When the doctor entered the room ready to commence the actual procedure, Elle closed her eyes and mentally counted down from five. She couldn't remember a time she had been this nervous. Her abdominal cavity was uncomfortably swollen due to the hormones and diet they had put her on. That was the worst part. The needle through the vagina wasn't great either. In the end, the doctor and nurse seemed optimistic and told her they'd know in a few days how many eggs had survived.

It was a pretty anti-climactic experience, to be honest.

An uncomfortable Elle walked silently out of the clinic toward Daria who waited in her car to take Elle home. What a weird feeling.

A piece of her had just been taken out, and by her own volition. She felt a bit of emptiness, though she realized she was planting a hopeful seed for her future. Part of her wanted to call Jane about it, but she decided not quite yet. She needed to digest her emotions a bit first. Her feelings were cradled by abdominal bloating the doctor said would take about a week to dissipate.

As she thought about her best friend, she was overcome with gratefulness. Jane was the one who had encouraged her to date seriously.

Elle reflected on her current life. The days of one-night stands were officially in her past and her future was looking bright. Her relationship with Daria, though new, was going well. At this point, Elle wasn't sure where things would lead. However, she could say with certainty that she was open to an actual relationship and that having a baby in the future was a definite possibility.

* * *

Tonight was the night.

Christine was going to talk to Paul. She had successfully called things off with Frankie earlier in the week. He'd been upset but calm, and asked her the "what about us?" question. Chris told him that she just couldn't do this to her family, that she wanted to make it work with her husband, and that she was so sorry she dragged him into it. In a surprising show of maturity, Frankie had replied he was happy to have spent the time with her but that even though he understood, he was still a little heartbroken and would need some distance at work for a while. His sad smile as he wished her luck burned in her memory, but Chris knew it was the right call.

Now she was focused on repairing her marriage. If that was even possible.

A thousand invisible insects crawled over her skin thinking about the upcoming conversation. She really didn't know if she was about to lose her marriage. Paul had continued working late nights and early mornings, but tonight she would wait up. Shutting this down with Frankie was the first step, but Paul had the right to know what she did, if he wanted to. If their marriage was going to work, they both needed to come clean, or at least agree to leave it all in the past.

As Paul walked in, Christine stood up. "Hi. I hope you had a good day at work. We … we really need to talk."

Her calmness seemed to throw him off kilter.

"Paul. I love you. But things have been off and I just … I think it's time we be really honest with each other."

His slight nod was all she needed. This was finally happening. There had been so much tension in the air lately, it was a welcome relief. She poured them each a glass of wine and they sat on the couch, facing each other.

"I'll start," she began. "I know we've drifted apart a lot, and I know that's as much my fault as it is yours. I'm sorry, I really am. But I feel unseen by you. You're never here, your kids miss you, I've been going to a gym and I've lost ten pounds and you haven't noticed. You're like a ghost."

Paul took in a deep breath. "I guess I've been … avoiding this. But yeah, I've been gone a lot on purpose. I don't know, Chris, I've been feeling so … stressed." Chris, nodded, ready to take it in. Paul continued. "I'm under a ton of pressure at work. And I don't love it. It makes me wonder if I chose the right career or not. And we've been off, I know we have. It just seems I can't do anything right. I just disappoint you. And the kids. God, I love them, but sometimes I don't know what to do with them. They just want their mom. I have nowhere that I just, you know, fit in."

"Wow. That's a lot," Chris said.

"As you know, I've been spending a lot of time at work with Angela."

Here it was.

"Paul. It's ok."

"We didn't ... I almost. I ... we came close, but I didn't. I didn't sleep with her." And for the first time, Chris believe that. It was written in the guilt and longing all over his face. He hadn't done it. "Ok. Are you ready to move on from her?"

"I am," Paul answered easily.

Chris inhaled. Her turn. "I had a fling. With someone at work. And I'm so sorry. But it's done now."

"Did you sleep with him?" Paul asked.

Christine knew he'd ask, so she'd come up with a strategy for this question. She really wanted to do right by her husband. But what Jane had said made sense. Why blow up their lives with guilt that would result in no action? Plus, Chris planned to find a therapist who could help her ultimately decide how much to tell him. For now, this was the only way she knew how to service her relationship.

"Almost," she said. She paused a beat. "Would you leave me if I had?"

Paul thought it out. "No. I wouldn't."

At least for now, she had done the right thing. The confession would have only hurt him, since he'd stay with her.

"So where do we go from here? What do you want to do?" she asked, her marriage hanging on the question.

"I want us to work," he said.

Thank God. Christine exhaled a breath she hadn't realized she'd been holding.

Paul continued and she listened. "I want you to understand when I have to work late, and I want to be home more. Maybe I want a different job. Still law, but a less stressful firm. I want ... I want you to tell me what to do with the kids. You're so good with them. And I'm not. And I want to be better. And I ... I want us to talk more. It's hard but it's ... it's good."

"I can do that," she whispered in his ear, hugging her husband as if her life depended on it.

"What do you need from me?" her husband asked, for the first time in a very long time.

"I need you to spend time with us. And I need you to see me, really see me and make me feel appreciated and loved. I will focus on us. And I want you to focus on us, too."

"I can do that," he said back through a thin veil of tears.

That night, for the first time in recent memory, the couple enjoyed each other physically and intimately. Holding each other and moving together in ways that felt so familiar, yet brand new. They finished together, caressing each other sweetly before falling asleep in each other's arms.

* * *

At around 2pm on Saturday, Jane pushed herself toward her car and asked Siri to take her to Braunger's Babies. She wanted to get there toward the end of the day. That way, if Ridgeley was willing to talk to her, she wouldn't be interrupting appointments.

Nerves set in as she pulled into the parking lot, seeing the tell-tale cat logo on the clinic's sign. She paused to catch her breath for a few seconds, then loudly yelled "Fuck it!" and got out of the car.

Upon entering the clinic Jane walked up to the Riley behind the counter and asked to speak with Dr. Braunger.

"What is this regarding?" the Riley asked.

"I…I'm an old friend," Jane lied.

Riley rose from her desk, a bit uncertain, and went to fetch Dr. Braunger.

As the veterinarian rounded the corner, Jane's chin dropped. Holy shit. It was really her. "Ridgeley?" she eeked out.

Ridge looked up, recognition immediately registering on her face.

"Oh my God, nobody calls me that anymore," Ridgeley replied. "Jane, what are you doing here?" It was a reasonable question. "Wait," Ridgeley added, "are you a serial killer? Should I be scared, because your showing up at my job is super weird and something a serial killer would do."

"No. Oh my God, nothing like that. I'm here about a painting. I mean, I'm here about a lot more. But not in a scary way." She ran her hands through her hair with a huff. "Look, I know this is insane, but can we talk?"

Ridgeley looked to the Riley who looked away, trying to hide her interest. "Ok. I have a consultation room open."

They walked to the room and suffered through an awkward thirty seconds before Jane broke the silence. "I have something I want to talk to you about but it's gonna take me a few minutes to work up the guts to get there. Is that ok?" Jane asked.

"I...ok," Ridgeley responded, visibly unsettled.

"So... *Wham!*, eh?" Ridgeley looked mortified, then laughed a bit. She copped to the history of the name immediately. Though Ridge had loved George Michael, the "other guy from Wham!" had been her childhood true love. "Yeah, I discovered Wham! on some MTV throwback show and became obsessed. I made my friends start calling me Mrs. Ridgeley in elementary school."

"Yikes," Jane responded, though Ridgeley was undeterred.

"The nickname died after few years, but when I got to college, I wanted to re-invent myself."

"Why?" Jane asked naively.

Ridgeley shifted uneasily. "You see Jane, my mother...my mother is Tiana Ferrawhey."

Jane did a spit take, despite drinking nothing. "WHAT?!" Holy shit, this was huge. "Tiana Ferrawhey, the hugely influential artist from the 70s? The woman who painted 'Fish out of Water' and one of my favorite artists? *That* Tiana Ferrawhey? How'd nobody known about that?"

"Because I didn't want them to. Growing up that's all I was; Tiana's daughter."

"So that's why Al and Mara wouldn't tell me more," Jane said under her breath.

"What?" asked Ridgeley.

"Nothing," Jane replied. "You were saying? About being Tiana Farrawhey's *daughter*?"

"Your reaction is the exact reason I never told anyone in college," Ridgeley went on with a wry smile.

Clocking Ridgeley's wedding ring, Jane realized Braunger was her married name. "Your maiden name is Geraldine Farrawhey?" she asked.

"No, actually. I originally had my dad's last name, Barnes. Even with that, the Ferrawhey-Barnes divorce was known well enough in the art world that had I gone with my real name, people would have asked questions."

She was right. Jane might not have known that Tiana's ex's last name was Barnes, but the art professors of UCLA certainly would have.

Ridgeley shifted a little. "These days the name Geraldine Barnes wouldn't ring many bells but at the time it was a bit different. The Internet was becoming a thing, and it seemed like people would find out. I didn't want my professors to know I was a legacy. I didn't want to have to live up to my mother's name, especially because I wasn't sure if I even had a passion for art."

"What are you talking about?" Jane interjected. "You were incredible. Your passion showed in your art all the time!"

"My mother made it nearly impossible for me to go for anything but art, but my heart wasn't in it. I agreed to major in it under one condition: my mom paid the university to maintain my anonymity. My professors didn't even know my real name. At that time, even the name 'Geraldine' would have raised questions for those really looped in to the art scene. But still, I could have picked a last name," she said depreciatingly. "I mean, what was I, Cher?"

Jane snorted. "That's what I always said. But wow. I love Tiana's…your mom's stuff. But…how weird for you?" Jane half-stated and half-asked.

"What always killed me was my mom would come up with

these crazy concepts of like, a top hat at a beret convention, and accurately show a fucking top hat's discomfort, yet she never saw mine. Hello, I was the fish out of water." Oh, wow. She had a point.

"Were you ever into it? Into art?" Jane asked.

Ridgeley paused. "I was. During the first two years of college I loved it. There was even a moment where I thought I could make a life out of it. But something changed." She looked at Jane, meaningfully.

"What?" Jane blurted out.

"Do you really not get it?" Ridgeley asked. Jane's blank expression gave a clear answer of 'nope.' "Jane, you. You're the reason I quit art."

OUCH. Fuck. "OUCH. Fuck," Jane said.

"No, not in a bad way. I wanted to quit. I didn't love it. You helped me realize that."

Jane sat stunned. "But like, how?"

Ridgeley explained. "I always admired the passion that went into your work. You felt it. It was your very essence."

Jane couldn't help but laugh at the floweriness. "Sorry, but I feel like I was never that cheesy about it."

"Really?" Ridgeley counted. "I once heard you say that you used art 'as a vehicle to show your true self to the world, and more importantly, to show it to yourself.'"

"Shit, I said that?" Jane asked, horrified.

"Yep."

Wow. Early college Jane was actually un-jaded. Until she jaded herself.

Ridgeley continued. "At first I tried to ignore it. But after that competition sophomore year, I couldn't do it anymore."

"Wait," Jane interrupted. "The same competition that made *me* quit art?"

Ridgeley nodded. "The depth of your painting took my breath away. It had the exact element my work was missing. When I won, I was furious." Wow. So was Jane. "At first I was afraid my professors discovered my mom, but they hadn't. It was worse. They thought mine was better. Or they assumed it was, just because I had won before. But they were so wrong, Jane. So wrong."

A tear came to Jane's eye. "This whole time, you thought I should've won?" Here Jane had been, blaming her own failures on Ridgeley, who had, in fact, been backing her since day one.

"Yes. So I quit. I couldn't stay in a department that had missed something so obvious."

"I... felt like such a failure back then. I thought I could never beat you."

Ridgeley paused. "You know Jane, I always thought it was strange that you were envious of me. You were the one who had it. You were an *artist*." Jane's tears flowed more freely. "I'm not an art person, I'm an animal person. I always have been. Remember when I came up to you and asked if I could have your painting?" Jane nodded through tears. "That's why. It was the very thing that allowed me to break out of my mother's spell and follow my true path. I dropped out of UCLA to study veterinary sciences at UC Davis."

This was information overload. "Are you saying I helped you?" Jane asked, stunned.

"You did. Your painting did. I had already been accepted to Davis, I just never thought I'd have the guts to go. My mother didn't speak to me for six months after that. Then one day she called me with a question about her cat, and we went from there."

The painting! "Actually, that painting is why I'm here."

"Really?" Ridgeley asked.

Jane started from the beginning. She talked about her grandmother, her extended 'break' from art, and her recent epiphanies. "You see, I blamed you. At least sort of. I resented the hell out of you because you had always gotten what I wanted. So, when my grandma said she wanted the painting, it was a done deal. I wanted to see where you ended up and to get my painting back. I wanted to look you in the face and try to take back what you took from me...even though I knew, I fucking knew, that stealing someone's life path wasn't a thing."

She told Ridgeley about the clues she'd picked up to track her down, and how each clue brought her closer to art and herself. And she even brought up Dave.

"Aw, you still talk to him?" Ridgeley asked.

"More like, I talk to him again."

"I only dated him for like a month but he talked about you all the time. It made me wonder if you guys had a thing going. That's one of the reasons I broke it off."

Wow. So, not only had Ridgeley *not stolen* Dave, she had actually tried to *return* Dave to Jane.

"Ridgeley, I'm sorry. I'm so sorry I was so jealous. I blamed you for so much shit, and it was all my fault. I thought you took from me. But really, in a sense you have helped give me my life back." The sentiment was so true, Jane wasn't even embarrassed by its floweriness.

"I still have the painting, you know."

"You do?" Jane asked, optimistic.

"Yeah. And given the history of it, I think you should have it back."

"Oh my God. Thank you. My grandma will be so happy! I'm so happy too." She paused. Ridgeley had already given her so much. "Are you sure?"

"I'm sure. It's served its purpose for me. Your grandma should have it."

"Is it as good as I remember?" Immediately regretting her conceit, Jane added, "Or whatever?"

"Why don't you tell me?" Ridgeley asked her receptionist to close up shop. She didn't have any more appointments that day and there was another doctor in the back in case any walk-ins came in. Ridgeley invited Jane to her car.

"Where are we going?" Jane asked.

"To my house." This was not how Jane had expected the day to go. She had thought that at worst, Ridgeley wouldn't remember her and would think she was a psychopath, and at best Ridgeley *would* remember her and think she was a psychopath. Never in her wildest daydreams did she see the woman inviting her to the house where her family lived.

After a few minutes, they pulled up to a tasteful one-story house with a stone façade and adobe siding. Jane hesitated to get out of the car. What if the painting was awful? What if for all these years she had built it up as this grand *pièce de résistance*, and it ended up being crap?

"Coming?" Ridgeley nudged her.

Ridgeley's house felt like a place kids could grow up knowing they'd be ok. The walls had neutral tones and the flooring was earthy.

Jane took in the art work adorning the walls: soft, melodic, ethereal. It was categorically Ridgeley. "I see you still dabble?"

Ridgeley blushed. "Yeah. Old habits die hard. And I do like art. It's a part of me, after all. I just don't love it enough to make a career out of it." She took Jane to a back room, which was clearly her office and looking around, Jane caught her breath.

On the back wall, framed above Ridgeley's desk, was her painting. "You hung it up?"

Ridgeley gave her an "are you an idiot?" look. "Have you not been listening? I told you, that painting is the reason I followed my path. I keep it where I can see it so I can remember where I'm going."

Jane took the painting in. She laughed as she realized that, technically speaking, it was not as great as she had remembered. Yet she would never call it mediocre. There was real depth to it. There were some things she'd clean up now if she could, but the raw emotion couldn't be topped. She felt a golf ball swell in her throat.

"It's ok," Ridgeley said. "I've cried over it too." She paused, adding, "I am sorry for any pain I helped cause you."

The two women stood there staring at the painting on the wall in stillness, taking it in. Jane began to lightly cry; a cathartic cry. She had come full circle and finally felt like she was back to where she needed to be.

"Here," Ridgeley offered as she moved to remove the painting from the wall. "This belongs to you."

"It feels weird now taking it. You've already given me everything I was looking for."

Ridgeley smiled. "It's your grandma's now."

Jane approached, half wanting to hug her and half wanting to give her a less connected high-five. She split the difference quite awkwardly, then the two women paused in silence.

"You know," Ridgeley began, "my mom owns a gallery in L.A. You're probably a bit out of practice but when you feel ready give me a call. I can't guarantee you a full show or anything, but I'm sure she'd be willing to show some of your work."

Jane's eyes filled with tears. Again. This was a gift that she in no way deserved. "Wow. That would be amazing."

The women exchanged contact information, and Ridgeley took Jane back to her car at the clinic.

"You know Ridge, I've got to say, this was so much more than I had hoped for. Thank you for everything, and I promise I won't stalk you again."

"Meh. I'd hardly call it stalking. More like tracking. And I'll be your Reese Witherspoon journey any day."

Jane pulled out her phone, wanting to share the good news but unsure who to text. Elle? Nah, she was probably out with Daria. Chris? I mean, she had enough going on these days. Plus, Jane had more to say than 'I found the painting.' And she finally felt ready to say it.

She pulled up Dave's number.

I found the painting. Can you come over tonight?

That evening, after dropping the painting off at her grandmother's, Jane re-raided her storage unit.

About an hour later, Dave walked through Jane's door, pizza in hand.

"I thought of bringing flowers, but I thought you'd think it was cheesy." He looked up to see Jane, working on a newly touched canvas. "Janey, are you painting?"

She looked at him, glowing. "Yeah. I'm just... I don't know, I felt inspired."

"It's gorgeous," he said sincerely.

"Thanks. It's a work in progress."

Putting the pizza down, Dave came up behind her.

"You know, you apologized to me but I never apologized to you," Dave began. "I messed up too. In college. I should have never dated Ridgeley when I had you standing right in front of me."

"Dave..." Jane began, but he stopped her.

"I'm so fucking happy you reached out to me."

They had an awkward but delicious moment of staring into each other's eyes, wondering who would flinch first. Then it happened. Dave leaned in ever so slightly and grazed Jane's lips with his. The grazing only lasted for a second until it devolved into feasting, making her breath catch and a moan rise in her throat, then slowed back to grazing. It was fucking amazing, and Jane was speechless. But in true Jane fashion, that didn't stop her from freaking out and talking.

"Dave, I..."

"Shh. Don't talk. I know you. Just, don't. Jane, I don't know what we have. I don't know if we'll end up friends or something much more but I want to find out, and I'm pretty sure you do too."

Shit, that was spot on. Jane smiled something huge and then made a move she'd wanted to make for a long time. She reached back and without warning, she grabbed Dave's ass with a fierceness that made him yell. She erupted in laughter. He faux pushed her, then grabbed her and pulled her in for their second, but not last, kiss.

THE END

Made in the USA
Las Vegas, NV
13 July 2021

26386795R00121